FIRE STORM

Lauren St John

Orion
Children's Books

First published in Great Britain in 2014
by Orion Children's Books
a division of the Orion Publishing Group Ltd
Orion House
5 Upper St Martin's Lane
London WC2H 9EA

1 3 5 7 9 10 8 6 4 2

A catalogue record for this book
is available from the British Library

Typeset by Input Data Services Ltd,
Bridgwater, Somerset

Printed and bound in Great Britain
by Clays Ltd, St Ives plc

ISBN 978 1 4440 0271 3

www.laurenstjohn.com
www.orionbooks.co.uk

For Catherine Clarke, who
routinely makes the impossible
possible, with love and a
thousand thanks

1

IN A CORNER stable at White Oaks Equestrian Centre, Casey Blue was experiencing an unfamiliar and distinctly unwelcome sensation – that of being crushed by a one-ton horse. For reasons unknown, Lady Roxanne had taken exception to being saddled and was expressing her displeasure by trying to paste Casey against the wall.

'Excuse me!' Casey panted indignantly after wriggling free. She massaged her ribs. 'That's no way for a lady to behave.'

In weeks to come Casey would discover that she was just one of a long line of people who routinely used that phrase – and worse – in connection with Roxy, but for now she was in the dark. She assumed that she'd inadvertently touched a sensitive spot on the horse's flank, or that Roxy was simply nervous in a new environment.

The 16.2hh bay mare had arrived the previous day when Casey was in London celebrating her father's birthday. It was especially important that she was with him because he'd only recently been released from prison for a crime he didn't commit. She'd asked her coach, Mrs Smith, to take care of things in her absence, but somehow that hadn't happened: when the lorry turned up neither Mrs Smith nor Casey had been there to welcome Storm's temporary replacement. Hardly surprising that Roxy was unimpressed.

Making encouraging noises, Casey reached for the girth. Roxy pinned her ears to her head, shifted her quarters and made a snapping noise with her teeth. She made it plain that if any attempt were made to fasten it, there would be consequences.

'Look, I know we've started out on the wrong foot, but I promise I'll make it up to you,' said Casey, leading the mare out into the yard where she was less likely to turn her new rider into a brick sandwich. 'You've obviously had a bad experience in the past, but it won't be like that here. I'm one of the good guys. Ask Storm.'

At the mention of Storm Warning, her champion horse, she felt a pang. She could see him in the far field, grazing peacefully with his friends. The other horses, mainly bays and a couple of chestnuts, blurred into one at this distance, but Storm's silver coat – the colour of

2

lightning blended with thundercloud was how Casey liked to think of it – set him apart from the crowd even on dull grey days like this one.

Usually he'd be at the gate as soon as he spotted her, as eager to go out for a gallop as he was for treats and love, but today he was enjoying his holiday. Casey didn't blame him. Barely two weeks had passed since they'd won the Badminton Horse Trials and Kentucky Three-Day Event back to back – a feat that had earned Casey a place in the record books as the youngest rider in history to complete the double.

It wasn't until the British Airways horse transport plane landed at London's Stansted airport at the end of a long, gruelling journey from the US that Casey had realised how exhausted she was. She was in bed and fast asleep within hours of arriving home at Peach Tree Cottage and didn't surface for nearly two days. Storm had done much the same, lying flat on his side and dreaming like a foal.

When at last Casey did emerge from her bedroom, she took a well-earned break. For twelve glorious days she rose late, read books and spent time with her dad, who'd been warmly welcomed back to his old job at the Half Moon Tailor Shop. His boss, Ravi Singh, had never doubted his innocence. Best of all were the long beach walks and romantic picnics that she enjoyed with Storm's farrier, Peter, who also happened to be her new boyfriend. She was so besotted with him that even the thought of him made the blood practically fizz in her veins.

Rested and restored ('rebooted' she'd joked to Peter), she was now ready for the season ahead. Her primary focus was the Burghley Horse Trials in September. Victory there would hand her eventing's greatest prize: the Rolex Grand Slam.

So ferocious was the competition for this triple that only one rider had ever achieved it: Pippa Funnell in 2003. Hers was a feat that could never be repeated, because she'd won Badminton, Kentucky and Burghley in the days when the long format, which included a steeplechase and roads and tracks, was still an integral part of any three-day event. Even without the extra mileage, no rider had managed it since, although Andrew Hoy, William Fox-Pitt and Andrew Nicholson had come close.

Casey, who considered the 'short format' of dressage, cross-country and show jumping tough enough, considered Pippa to be some kind of superhero. At seventeen, she was years away from being anywhere near as good as Pippa, but miracles did happen – especially when you had a horse like Storm Warning. And Casey had the Badminton and Kentucky trophies to prove it!

The only cloud on the horizon was that Storm needed to have six weeks' rest before being brought back into training. Hence Roxy. Casey had imagined that, on the back of her success in Gloucestershire and Kentucky, she'd have her choice of top horses to ride for a couple of months, until Storm was once more ready for action. But with less than a week to go before she was due to resume work, nobody had come forward with a suitable mount.

Morag, White Oaks' acerbic manager, was unsympathetic. 'What did you expect? Your achievements this season are phenomenal, Casey Blue, and as a friend I'm in awe of you, but I wouldn't want you or Mrs Smith within a mile of one of my up-and-coming horses. Your unconventional – some would say downright batty – training methods are already the stuff of legend.'

'They can't be that batty,' protested Casey. 'Our results speak for themselves.'

'Yes, but not everyone wants their horse ridden flat out along a public beach without a bridle, or paddled in their neighbour's swimming pool. And those were among your more sensible experiments.'

Unfortunately, Morag was right. No one else was blunt enough to say it to their faces, but the end result was the same: a distinct lack of offers of shiny warmbloods with impressive CVs. That didn't bother Mrs Smith, because from the outset she was fixated on getting a youngster.

'In a perfect world what we need is a novice eventer who is still pretty green. Something to challenge us.'

'What *I* need,' said Casey, 'is a two-star, or even a three-star horse with a proven track record in show jumping and dressage so I'll be able to stay competitive throughout the season.'

'And what is this paragon of a creature going to teach you? What are you going to learn? Might I remind you that, Storm aside, you have only ever ridden one horse, and there'd be those who'd argue that Patchwork was at least three parts mule. The best riders on the circuit have ridden dozens of horses. They've also ridden and competed in many different arenas, from Pony Club competitions to local hunts and amateur racing. That's how great riders hone their skills. That's how they learn what makes horses tick.'

Casey, who was keenly aware that she lacked the riding experience that even the lowliest competitor on the circuit took for granted, said nothing.

Next day she was offered a couple of wildly unsuitable show jumpers by an ambitious couple who boarded their horses at White Oaks.

Just as she was beginning to despair, she'd received an email about Lady Roxanne, an Irish sporthorse who'd achieved reasonable results at intermediate level. Her owner, Jennifer Stewart, claimed that the mare had bags of potential but consistently underperformed. She begged Casey to consider taking her on. *As Badminton and Kentucky champion, you are among the world's best young riders and will undoubtedly help her to realise her potential,* she gushed in one email.

In another to Mrs Smith, she described Roxy as *gifted but challenging*.

Casey hadn't liked the sound of that at all.

'It has an ominous ring to it. Jennifer Stewart is like an estate agent describing a house as a dream home but needing a little work. I'll move in and discover that it's a crumbling ruin.'

6

Her teacher shook her head in wonder. 'Would you listen to yourself? Are you the same girl who, less than three years ago, paid a dollar for a bag-of-bones horse from a knacker's yard and shaped him into one of Britain's finest eventers? Now you're turning up your nose at a well-bred mare who has extensive competition experience just because her owner describes her as a little challenging?'

'She didn't use the word "little", said Casey, but she knew she was clutching at straws. And Mrs Smith did have a point. Taking on a mare who was a bit of a project could be both rewarding and educational. It might also distract her from missing Storm.

'You're right, as usual. I do need to ride more horses and this is the perfect opportunity for me to really get to know and understand a horse with a totally different tempcrament from Storm. Now that I think about it, I can't wait to get started.'

Recalling these words, Casey led Roxy to the hitching post in the yard. She stood for a moment admiring her new mount. The mare was the colour of toffee, with a shiny black mane and lustrous, intelligent eyes. When she wasn't scowling and snapping, she was pretty.

Distracted by the change of scene, Roxy stood perfectly still even when Casey adjusted the saddle. Her expression was positively serene. Casey relaxed. The crushing episode in the stable was obviously an aberration. Reaching for the girth, she started to pull it tight.

'Ow!'

Her screech of pain was so loud that it scared the birds from the nearby trees. Roxy had nipped her left arm, drawing blood.

As Casey swore beneath her breath and rubbed the purple flesh, she was shocked to see that Roxy's ears were pricked. The mare was staring into the distance as if the whimpering girl at her side was as inconsequential as a swatted fly.

Casey was relieved that the yard was empty and there was no one around to witness her humiliation. All the instructors were taking lessons and Morag and a couple of the stable girls were at a show. She glanced at her watch in annoyance. Where on earth was Mrs Smith? Her teacher had disappeared to Brighton the previous day on a mysterious errand and was now an hour and a half late, poor form when it was their first lesson back after a break and they had a tricky new horse to train. Casey had waited as long as she could before the delicious prospect of trying out her new mare had got the better of her.

If Mrs Smith had been a normal teacher, she could have rung her for an ETA, but Mrs Smith loathed mobile phones and had yet to answer the one Casey had bought her on their return from the US. That meant that Casey was on her own with the ironically named *Lady Roxanne*.

Adopting what she hoped was a stern but kindly tone, she explained to Roxy that biting, kicking and pasting riders against walls were all unacceptable behaviour at White Oaks. The mare ignored her. Casey lifted the saddle flap cautiously and put a wary hand on the girth. Nothing happened. But as she leaned in to tighten it, Roxy's head whipped round and she went for the kill, biting Casey so hard on the bum that she leapt into the air with a squeal.

An explosive laugh startled them both. Casey squinted into the shadows. A stranger was leaning against the stable-block wall. He was so close it seemed impossible that she hadn't seen him, and yet with his black polo-shirt, dark brown breeches and black long boots he was all but invisible in the shade.

He straightened unhurriedly and stepped into the sunlight. Casey caught her breath. He was shorter than Peter – perhaps by as much as two inches – and was as fair as her boyfriend was dark, but he had the kind of looks that teen magazines call 'heart-stopping'.

'I think you'll find that if you give her a carrot next time she does that, she'll be so surprised that it'll diffuse her temper,' he said in a friendly tone. 'She'll try to nip you again, of course, but if you respond by offering her another carrot, she'll soon learn that what she's come to regard as a negative experience is really rather fun.'

What he said made sense, but Casey's hackles rose. She didn't appreciate being told what to do by a boy she didn't know from Adam, especially a good-looking one and when she was in pain. 'Is that so?' she said coldly.

He flashed a grin and his hand came up and swept

streaky blond hair out of his eyes. 'But I'm sure you already know that. You don't get to achieve what you've achieved, especially with a horse as complex and brilliant as Storm Warning, without having rare gifts of communication with animals.'

Casey immediately felt silly for having taken offence over something so trivial when he'd clearly been trying to help. Besides, anyone who praised Storm was all right by her. She smiled. 'Oh, I wouldn't go that far. My horse-whispering skills are really not working on Roxy.'

'Wanna try the carrot trick?'

Casey hesitated, but her arm and right buttock were killing her and she didn't fancy being chomped again. 'Why not?'

When Roxy swung round with her teeth bared, Casey surprised her by popping a carrot in her mouth. Roxy was too busy crunching to worry about the girth or anything else. With the help of another two carrots, Casey was able to adjust the bridle unmolested.

'Need a leg up?'

Casey hesitated. The mounting block was at the far end of the yard. She'd finally got Roxy settled. Maybe it would be better to mount her now while she was quiet. 'Sure. Uh, thanks.'

As the visitor moved to cup his hands beneath her boot, his bicep brushed her chest. Casey felt a shot of pure attraction go through her, followed, almost immediately, by an inexplicable feeling of dread and guilt. The combined feelings disturbed her so much that she lost concentration and almost flew over the other side of Roxy.

'Don't mind me, I'm here for my first riding lesson,' she joked, struggling back into the saddle, red-faced.

'It was entirely my fault,' he said graciously. 'Don't know my own strength. Believe me, no one would ever mistake you for an amateur, Casey Blue.'

Casey gathered the reins. Now that she was gazing down on him, she felt more in control. It also occurred to her that there was something familiar about him. 'You obviously know my name. Mind telling me yours?'

'Apologies. I seem to have left my manners at home today. I'm Kyle. It's a pleasure to finally meet you. It's something I've wanted for a very long time.'

He said it as if he'd thought of nothing else for months.

'Why?' Casey asked before she could stop herself.

He grinned. 'Why not? You're the hottest young rider in the country.'

As he reached up to shake her hand, some sixth sense warned Casey that nothing good would come out of any association with him. She dragged her eyes away from his dark blue ones and glanced at the distant gate. Where *was* Mrs Smith?

Casey kept her voice cool. 'I'm hardly that, but thanks. You event?'

'Heavens, no. Not brave enough. On the whole, I find the ground a lot safer. Fewer broken bones. I teach a bit.'

It was then that the penny dropped. Casey hid her astonishment by allowing the restless mare to move forward a few paces. She could have echoed his compliment by saying, 'I know who you are. You're the hottest coach in Britain.' But there was something in the confident set of his shoulders that told her he already knew that. The previous October he had, at twenty, been the youngest person ever to be shortlisted for the Golden Horseshoe Riding Instructor of the Year Award, before being controversially beaten to the title. The eventing circuit had been abuzz with rumours about it afterwards. Since the winner was a close relative of one of the judges, the general consensus was that the result had been fixed and Kyle robbed.

She reined in Roxy. 'You're Kyle West?'

Again the laconic grin. 'Last time I checked.'

'Here to give someone a lesson?'

He stepped forward and pushed his blond fringe from his face as he looked up at her. 'Actually, I was hoping to see you.'

'Me?'

'Yes, I'd like a word with you if that's possible.'

Casey was as curious as a cat in a den of mice, but she didn't want to seem too eager. 'No problem at all, provided you don't mind hanging around for an hour or so. As you've probably gathered, Roxy and I are just getting to know one another and my coach, Mrs Smith, who should be here, isn't.'

Kyle kept pace with them as they left the yard. 'Sure

thing. Would it be okay if I watched you work? I mean, I don't want to intrude.'

'Be my guest,' said Casey, not knowing that those three words, so carelessly spoken, would change everything.

2

DESPITE THE LOW-SLUNG banks of cloud there was a brightness to the day, and the outdoor ménage, set against a backdrop of wildflowers, sheep and the five-hundred-year-old oaks that gave the stables their name, had seldom looked so inviting. Still Casey chose the indoor school, which afforded a little more privacy.

If Kyle thought it an odd choice, he made no comment. Without being asked, he settled himself on one of the tiered wooden benches that provided seating during winter competitions, sitting so still and silent that he was once again all but invisible.

At first his presence made Casey self-conscious, but the joy of being back in the saddle on a willing horse soon superseded that. Jennifer Stewart had not been exaggerating. Roxy had talent in spades. Her quarters needed serious work, but on the whole she was a beautiful mover. Tacking up aside, the only challenge so far had been staying aboard during a light-hearted bout of bucking.

As the session proceeded, Casey's confidence grew. She felt pleased that Kyle was there to witness her riding well and bonding with Roxy. It made up for the embarrassing scene in the yard. At the same time, it felt odd to be on a horse that wasn't Storm. Roxy didn't have Storm's power or fluidity or his almost psychic ability to read her mind, but she was responsive and there was plenty of pleasure to be had from her genuine paces. She had a good jump on her too, flying over a couple of low uprights as if she was at Hickstead. It was hard to believe that this was the same animal who, just minutes earlier, had drawn blood.

Kyle, for his part, said nothing. He leaned forward with a slight frown on his face, light rippling across his golden head as he turned to follow her progress. A couple of times she noticed him glancing down at his phone, but when she passed him again she appeared to have his full attention.

'Any comments?' called Casey as she slowed Roxy to a walk.

'You're doing great. Fantastic. I mean, there are a couple of tiny things but they're so tiny they're not even worth mentioning.'

Casey circled back. 'Mention away. What tiny things?'

'Really, they're nothing.'

'Then they shouldn't be hard to fix. Go on.'

'It's just – do you always do that thing with your foot?'

'What thing?'

'Put your weight on the outside of the stirrup so that you're leaning into your lower toe?'

For the second time that day, Casey felt like a beginner. 'What? No. I mean, I don't think so. Is that what I appear to be doing?'

He shrugged. 'It might not feel that way, but trust me, it is. It's so subtle that it's barely noticeable on the flat, but if you were jumping it would have the effect of destabilising your lower leg. Not exactly ideal if you're flying over the Cottesmore Leap at Burghley.'

Casey knew the fence well. She'd studied the television footage of it the previous year. It was the largest eventing fence in the world, its proportions exaggerated by the ditch that followed it, a yawning cavern so terrifying that, when walking the course prior to cross-country day, many riders chose to avoid it in case they lost their nerve before they'd even begun.

'Don't worry. It's easy enough to fix. Stand up in your stirrups until you feel balanced. See how your weight naturally inclines towards the inside? Now try it at a walk, trot and canter. There you go, you look better already. Feel any different?'

'Yes,' admitted Casey. She didn't want to say that in the entire three years she'd worked with Mrs Smith, her teacher had never spotted this apparently critical flaw.

'Try her over the oxer and see if it improves things.'

Casey did as he said and continued on over the upright. The difference was astounding. She felt so much more connected to Roxy, so much more secure. The mare seemed to make a better shape over the jumps too.

Kyle clapped. 'You're such a natural. Most of my pupils would take weeks to adopt a change like that.'

Casey halted in front of him. 'Anything else? You said there were a couple of things.'

He laughed. 'Oh, no, that's enough to be going on with for one day. I feel embarrassed to have said anything at all. You're the Badminton and Kentucky champion. You certainly don't need any tips from me. Really, Casey, I'm a massive fan.'

Casey found herself blushing. 'Thanks. Uh, if you bear with me for another ten minutes, we can have that talk you wanted.'

Elated, she urged Roxy into a canter. The mare popped neatly over the upright and turned towards the oxer. Her ears pricked and she put on a sudden burst of speed. At the last conceivable second, she slammed on the brakes.

Casey shot forward as if she'd been launched from a cannon, arms and legs flailing. She caught a brief glimpse of Kyle moving forward in slow motion and had time to cringe inwardly. Then she bellyflopped into the dirt, like a frog being dropped from a great height. For several minutes she was incapable of doing anything but gasp for air. Everything hurt, particularly her ribs and her bitten arm and buttock. But her primary sensation was humiliation.

Kyle came over with Roxy and helped her to her feet.

'Any advice?' Casey asked when she could finally speak.

Kyle grinned. 'Never get on any horse that hasn't first accepted you on the ground.'

After she'd tended to Roxy, who mercifully inflicted no further wounds, Casey walked Kyle to the car park.

'I'm sorry you had to see that. Deeply embarrassing.'

He laughed. 'Don't be daft. Even the best riders get taken by surprise now and then. She's a bit of a handful, Miss Roxy, but if anyone can take her to the next level it's you.'

Casey stopped. 'I wish I could share your optimism. Now what is it that you wanted to talk to me about?'

He looked down, dark lashes shadowing his cheeks. 'I ... okay, I'm now wondering if this is a terrible idea. You see, I'm here on the basis of a persistent rumour.'

'What rumour?'

'The talk on the circuit is that Mrs Smith is about to retire. I know it's presumptuous but I wondered if you'd do me the honour of letting me coach you. You're more than capable of winning the Burghley Horse Trials this year and I'd like to be the teacher who takes you there.'

Casey was stunned. 'I don't know what I expected you to say, but it wasn't that. I mean, I'm flattered that you'd offer to coach me, but you have it all wrong. People have always misjudged Mrs Smith because of her age, but if you knew her you'd know that, though she's in her sixties, she's smarter, stronger and more energetic and youthful than most twenty-year-olds ... '

She paused as a bus rattled around the corner and wheezed to a noisy stop in front of the riding centre.

'She's as healthy as an ox and would never dream of packing it in ... '

The bus door hissed open. Out stepped Mrs Smith. She stumbled slightly as her right foot touched the ground, tottered and almost fell. When she straightened, her skin was ghostly white and she looked every one of her sixty-three years. Her Indian cotton top and trousers, usually immaculate, looked crumpled, and it seemed to Casey that as she walked up the drive she wavered slightly in the breeze.

'Good morning all,' she called brightly. 'So sorry I'm late, Casey. Public transport nightmare.'

Kyle turned away to unlock a forest green MG sports car. His expression said all there was to say. 'Right, Casey, I'll be off. No point in troubling you further.' He pressed a business card into her hand. 'It's been a pleasure. Call if you need me.'

Casey avoided his eyes. 'I won't, but thanks.'

Perhaps it was the power of suggestion but as she gave

her teacher a hug it seemed to her that Mrs Smith felt thin to the point of being frail.

'Who was that?' Mrs Smith asked as the MG reversed smartly out of the yard.

Casey shut her ears to the thrilling growl of the sports car's engine as it powered away down the lane.

'Nobody important.'

her former mistress. It seemed to her that Mrs Smith felt...
...
while ... as it also with...been in the ...
...
...
...
...

3

CASEY WAS EIGHT years old when she first decided to become an eventer. She could recall the moment vividly. At the time, she was lying on the threadbare sofa at number 414 Redwing Towers, the East London council flat she shared with her father, re-reading a pony book for the zillionth time and breathing in the wafting delight of some soon-to-be-served vegetarian dinner. A small television crackled quietly in one corner.

'Five minutes till lift-off, Case,' called her father, which was her cue to stop reading and start laying the table. Casey didn't stir. She was in an exciting bit. She knew the outcome of the story, knew perfectly well that the foal would be saved from a snowy fate, but her heart still pounded.

'Casey Blue, where are you?' sang her father.

'Coming, Dad,' said Casey, eyes still glued to the page.

Two chapters later, she reluctantly set the book aside and hopped up. As she did so, another horse caught her attention – this one on the television. He was the fittest horse she'd ever seen and the same could be said for his rider. Galloping along a route lined with spectators, they were a perfect unit of power and grace. An enormous brush fence loomed. The horse popped over it as if it were nothing.

Casey sat down again.

As he rounded the kitchen bench with two plates of steaming lasagne, Roland Blue opened his mouth to chivvy her again. He shut it when he saw what had captivated her. Casey's mum had died when Casey was just two years old and ever since then horses – those in books and on television, those ridden by police in the street, and the shaggy cobs and ponies seen through the fence of the local riding school – had been her greatest comfort. As far as Roland was concerned, that was something to be encouraged. He grabbed some cutlery and a couple of napkins and sat down beside her.

'What are we watching? Oh, good, it's highlights from past Badminton Horse Trials. Don't know much about the event, but I do know that it's among the toughest sporting competitions on earth. Part of the reason is the death-defying fences. There's one of them right there! Did they really just jump over a house? Oh my goodness, when they clipped that log I was convinced they were going to come crashing down.'

'So was I,' gasped Casey.

'Yes, but from what I understand the real challenge of Badminton is finding a horse and rider that can multitask. It's a mix of dressage, which is a bit like horse ballet, cross-country and show jumping.'

'Wow. You'd need a horse with wings.'

'Indeed you would.'

As if to prove her right, horse and rider flew over a rustic post and rails and dropped off a virtual cliff. The camera angle made it seem nothing short of suicidal. The pair plummeted to earth, freefalling.

'Good grief,' said Roland Blue.

But the horse not only lived to tell the tale, he did so with feet neatly aligned and ears pricked. As he bounded forward with a cheeky swish of his tail, his rider, who Casey would later learn was Lucinda Green en route to one of her six Badminton wins, patted him ecstatically, a wide grin on her face.

Casey had been so overcome that it was a couple of minutes before she could get it together to speak. When she did, it was with a degree of conviction only possible if you're an eight-year-old yet to be confronted with the harsh realities of life without money or connections.

'That's going to be me some day.'

That day had been close to a decade coming. Now, as she sat at her laptop in the kitchen at Peach Tree Cottage, browsing through fan mail, Casey wondered if she'd have quit and pursued a less brutal career path had she known the challenges before her. Perhaps she should have tried to get into art school or become a veterinary nurse.

But even as the thought crossed her mind, her gaze was drawn to an old photograph stuck on the fridge. It was of her thirteen-year-old self, beaming in charity-shop breeches and a Hope Lane T-shirt. She smiled at the memory. There was no better reminder that if horses had been her passion before she started volunteering at the run-down Hackney riding school nicknamed Hopeless Lane, they'd quickly become her whole world. After she and her father saved Storm, skeletal and crazed with terror, from certain death at a knacker's yard, Casey's destiny had been sealed. From that day forward she knew that the only life she wanted was one that had her beloved silver horse at its heart.

Three years on, Casey had everything she'd ever dreamed of and more. She'd won two of the world's greatest equestrian championships and moved from abject poverty to relative wealth in six months. Starting out on the circuit, she, Storm and Mrs Smith had travelled in a broken-down rattletrap of a van more usually used to transport three woolly donkeys. Casey had dressed in second-hand breeches, shirts and jackets, and Storm had to endure ill-fitting tack borrowed from Hopeless Lane.

These days almost every new delivery brought cellophane-packed clothes, gleaming boots and the very best in horse feed and tack from generous sponsors. Only that morning Casey had checked her email to find a letter from a company who wanted to provide her with a luxury lorry with her name on the side. Casey, whose usual mode of transport was White Oaks' functional but basic horsebox, had been overjoyed. Without consulting Mrs Smith, who was her unofficial manager as well as her coach, she'd pinged off an email to say, 'Yes! Yes! Yes! Thank you! Thank you! Thank you!'

So life was good, not least because on top of these achievements she had a boyfriend who loved her, an adorable cottage home and great training facilities.

And yet deep down she wasn't happy.

Something was wrong. Something was niggling at her. The kitchen had always been Casey's favourite room in Peach Tree Cottage because it was cosy and smelled comfortingly of apple pie, but that afternoon it seemed unnaturally gloomy and cold. Casey couldn't decide if it was Kyle's visit and the disquieting effect he'd had on her that had set her nerves on edge, or if it was something else entirely. Whatever it was, it didn't feel good.

She glanced down at her laptop. There were 181 unanswered emails. Most were from young fans inspired by her achievements. Some were so complimentary they made her blush. The rest were mainly appeals from would-be sponsors and journalists. All good news and reasons to celebrate, so why did she feel so uneasy?

Casey slammed closed her laptop and pushed back her chair. Locking the kitchen door, she set off across the fields. This was Kyle's fault. If he hadn't sent her into a flat spin by suggesting that Mrs Smith was on the verge of retiring, she'd be as dreamily content as she had been first thing that morning.

As soon as her teacher had put down her bag and had a reviving cup of chai, Casey had asked her outright if she was planning to quit for health reasons. True to form, Mrs Smith had laughed.

'My dear, I might have to change the habits of a lifetime and start wearing more make-up. Clearly I'm looking peakier than I'd supposed.'

Casey was annoyed. 'Can you be serious for once? Over the past few months, you've had quite a few headaches and bouts of tiredness and pain, plus there were a couple of days in Kentucky when you looked really unwell.'

Mrs Smith stared at her incredulously. 'Are you joking? It was sweltering in Kentucky. The Sahara Desert would have felt cool by comparison. And on top of that we were being targeted by blackmailers. Anyone could be forgiven for feeling under the weather. As for the tiredness, *you* had a break after Kentucky. I didn't. I climbed off the plane and got straight to work, with jetlag. For most of the past two weeks I've been tying up sponsorship deals, dealing with the media and organising your replacement horse. May I remind you that I am sixty-three. I'm fit for my age but I'm not superwoman.'

She had a point, but Casey was reluctant to let it go.

'Does that mean you're thinking of retiring?'

'Do you *want* me to retire? Is that what this is about – you thinking that I'm over the hill and should be replaced?'

'Don't be ridiculous,' said Casey. 'That's the silliest thing I've ever heard. I only worry that you've been working too hard, that's all. You, Dad and Peter are the most important people on earth to me. Your health means more than any event anywhere, including Burghley. Promise that you'll be honest with me if you ever get ill. Promise that you'll tell me if you have so much as a sniffle.'

Mrs Smith gave her a hug. 'My dear, you and Storm are my whole world and what a beautiful world it is. I give you my word that if teaching ever gets too much for me, I'll tell you. But I'm not about to retire, that I can assure you, and I can promise I'll be at Burghley in September to see you win. Now talk to me about Lady Roxanne. How did you get on with her this morning?'

Storm was waiting by the field gate, keen to have his dinner. He whickered joyfully when he saw his mistress. As Casey led him to the yard, she tried not to think about the fact that despite her assurances of wellbeing, Mrs Smith had disappeared to her room for a couple of hours that afternoon. She'd claimed that she wanted to research a few techniques that would help them in the coming weeks, but when Casey passed her door the total silence emanating from it suggested she was sleeping.

An image of Kyle's handsome young face swam into Casey's head. He had charisma and an energy that contrasted unfavourably with the picture Mrs Smith had presented as she'd stumbled off the bus that morning. Kyle hadn't had to research techniques. It was clear that, despite his youth, he had all the equestrian knowledge he needed at his fingertips. The tip he'd given her on tacking up Roxy had worked a treat, and she couldn't wait to jump Storm again now that her foot and leg position had improved. It was a subtle thing, but she had a feeling it would make a big difference, particularly over Burghley's cardiac-arrest-inducing fences.

She hadn't mentioned Kyle's impromptu lesson to Mrs Smith, let alone that he'd tried to poach her. What would be the point? Mrs Smith was her best friend, not just her teacher. It was inconceivable that Casey could ever be coached by anyone else. They were a team.

Storm nudged her. Casey blinked. She'd led him to his stable on automatic pilot and, rather than attending to his needs, had spent several long minutes staring blankly into space. She gave him a cuddle and immediately her mood lifted. Storm appreciated her, even if Roxy didn't.

She kissed him on his velvet muzzle. 'All right, impatient. One gourmet dinner coming up.'

She was smiling as she walked to the feed room.

Rounding the corner, she saw Roxy gazing imperiously from her stable door. Casey stopped to stroke her, but the mare ducked away, ears back. Casey's smile faded.

'Excuse me, Casey Blue?'

Casey turned to see a couple of little girls in grubby breeches and matching pigtails. The taller one thrust out a glittery pink notebook.

'Please may we have your autograph?' she asked shyly.

Casey wiped her hands on her jeans. 'Of course you can.' She took the proffered pink pen. 'What are your names?'

As she wrote, the girls kept up a running commentary.

'We're your number one fans!'

'We want to win Badminton before we're eighteen, like you!'

'And the Kentucky Three-Day Event and the Burghley Horse Trials! We want to win them all!'

'We'll take it in turns!'

'We think Storm is the most magnificent horse that ever lived. He's a magical colour too. He looks like horse-shaped lightning.'

Casey couldn't suppress a grin. 'That's a lovely way of putting it. I think that too. He does look good on the outside but it's what's on the inside that makes him special.'

'Do you have any riding tips for us?'

'I have two. Number one: love your horse and always do what's right for him or her. Number two: never give up on your dreams.'

As they hurried away, giggling excitedly, Casey was reminded of a conversation she'd had with Peter the previous week. She'd been describing the moment when, as a pony-mad eight-year-old, she'd fallen in love with eventing.

'Has it been everything you thought it might be?' Peter had asked. 'I mean, when you were volunteering at Hopeless Lane and trying to train Storm, is this what you wanted – to be considered one of the top riders and to experience all the fame and glory that comes with it?'

'Of course it is,' Casey responded, laughing. 'What kind of question is that? Of course this is what I wanted. It's what I *do* want. Wouldn't anyone? I'm the luckiest girl in the world.'

As she walked back to Storm's stable, a bucket in each hand, Casey told herself again that that was exactly what she was – the luckiest girl in the world.

Wasn't she?

4

CASEY HAD TAKEN it for granted that Roxy would improve upon acquaintance, but she was wrong. On the surface, the mare was a dream. She was superbly bred and had great conformation and elegant paces. If she was in the right mood, she was surprisingly bold over White Oaks' cross-country course and capable of performing a sweet dressage test and clearing a field of show jumps.

But therein lay the rub. She would only do those things if it suited her. If it didn't, there was no telling what punishment she had in store for Casey. After ten days of riding her, Casey was purple from head to toe. She'd fallen off six times, been bitten three times, had both feet stepped on and suffered a repeat of the wall-crushing incident. Her injuries had become something of a joke around the yard.

'Why don't you keep a first-aid kit in Roxy's stable and be done with it?' teased Morag. 'I mean, there are stuntmen who work on James Bond films with less aches and pains.'

Renata, a lumpen stable girl, was more blunt. 'I thought you and old Mrs Smith fancied yourselves as horse-whisperer types. Your methods don't seem to be working on Lady Roxanne, do they? She seems to have a grudge against you. Maybe you should give Kyle West a call. They say that what he doesn't know about riding and horses isn't worth knowing. And oh my *God* is he cute.'

She fanned herself, as if Kyle's heat was steaming her up from afar.

Casey ignored her. She'd never forgiven Renata for allowing two strange men to snatch Storm one bleak winter's evening in February. The men did have the correct documentation and it wasn't exactly Renata's fault, but Casey had never really got over it.

Nonetheless, her own failure to win Roxy over was galling and it didn't help that her teacher found the whole thing funny. For some reason, it amused Mrs Smith that the mare consistently outsmarted them. It wasn't that Roxy reared or went crazy in order to unseat Casey. She did none of those things. Ninety-five per cent of the time she was well-behaved to the point of being angelic.

No, what was really disconcerting was that there was a degree of cunning involved. She'd clear seven jumps in a row, ears pricked, cantering beautifully, and then on the eighth, stop dead. Launched into space, Casey would often clear the jump on her own. There seemed no way to predict or prevent it.

Roxy's other favourite trick was to wait until Casey was relaxed in the saddle, reins loose, as they returned to the yard. She'd then shy at some imagined menace, leaping sideways so hard and fast that there was no physical way of Casey remaining in the saddle. Like a character in a Thelwell cartoon, Casey would hover momentarily in mid-air before crashing to the ground.

Somehow the sight of Mrs Smith falling about laughing made the pain worse. 'I'm sorry,' her coach spluttered when it happened for the third day running. At the time, Casey was returning to the yard after a relatively successful attempt at the cross-country course. 'It's just that … It's just … '

'What?' Casey demanded, clambering to her feet and biting back a groan. The pain radiating from her rear brought tears to her eyes. Nearby, Roxy munched grass unconcernedly.

Mrs Smith sobered up. 'I'm sorry. It's just that it's been decades since I came across such an intelligent animal. She's toying with us. My guess is that she's been abused or treated poorly in her past – not necessarily by Jennifer Stewart, who seems terribly well-intentioned, but someone else further down the line. A groom, perhaps.

33

There is no doubt in my mind that she's been put in a situation where she's felt powerless. She's learned that the only way to get revenge is to use her wits to make humans suffer.'

'But can't she understand that we're not like that?' Casey said crossly. 'I mean, since she's arrived I've bent over backwards to be lovely to her, even though she's been a total minx at times. In return, I've been thrown, bitten, kicked and stamped on. Whatever she's been through, it's nothing compared to the abuse Storm endured and yet he understood from the beginning that we loved him and were doing our best for him.'

'First things first: Storm is not Roxy. Comparing them will get you nowhere at all.'

'Yes, but—'

'Secondly, you need to understand that Roxy is testing you. It's not a test you can afford to fail. There is no secret to passing it, but there is a shortcut. Kindness. No matter what question she asks you or how many times she throws you, you respond with love and gentleness. That doesn't mean you should be a pushover. You're a team and she needs to understand her part in that.'

'Okay, so tell me how to do that. Teach me the right way to handle her.'

'I can't. This is *your* journey. I can teach you technique, but you're going to have to figure Roxy out for yourself. Think of her as being a bit like a Japanese secret puzzle box. You'll solve one mystery and then find yourself facing another. The mistake many riders make with

34

these types of horses is that they lose patience and force the issue. Try that with Roxy and it will backfire spectacularly. Attempt to dominate her and you'll make things a thousand times worse. You'll unlock the box with kindness, nothing else.'

Casey dusted down her breeches. 'That's all very well, but in a few days' time we'll be competing at the Salperton Horse Trials. If I haven't solved the mystery that is Roxy by then, we're going to be finishing last. Take what happened today. She shied at nothing. If she was afraid, I'd understand. But she's perfectly relaxed. It's all a game to her.'

She stopped. 'What is it? What's wrong?'

Her teacher's face, usually quite radiant, had gone puce. She clutched her side.

Casey dropped Roxy's reins and rushed over to her. 'Angelica, you're scaring me. Talk to me. What is it? Are you ill?'

Mrs Smith straightened up slowly, refusing Casey's arm. She smiled. 'Sorry about that. That sandwich we had for lunch didn't agree with me. I think the cheese might have been past its sell-by date.'

'I don't believe you. Are you ill, or aren't you? Either there's something you're not telling me or I'm dragging you to the doctor for tests.'

The colour had returned to Mrs Smith's cheeks. 'Oh for goodness' sake, Casey, sometimes you sound even more ancient than I do. Stop fussing. I'm not going to waste the doctor's time just because I have a spot of indigestion. At worst, I might be coming down with a cold.'

She scooped up Roxy's reins and handed them to her charge. 'If I were you I'd spend less time worrying about imaginary illnesses and more time focusing on Roxy. That's where your real challenge lies.'

Hobbling to the yard, rubbing her new bruises, Casey couldn't help noticing that Roxy's ears were pricked and she was stepping out keenly. The mare's mood always seemed to lift if she managed to unseat her new rider. Casey knew that Mrs Smith was right. The only way to change Roxy was to be patient and continue to try to bond with her. All the same, she would have appreciated some advice from the teacher she was paying to advise her. Kyle West had spent a sum total of forty minutes at White Oaks and yet he'd offered her several clear and helpful tips.

For free.

'Believe it or not, I am doing my best,' Casey told Roxy as she unsaddled her. 'Give me a chance and I'll prove that I'm worthy of your trust.'

She reached into her pocket for a packet of Polo mints. The mare hesitated for a long moment before gently lipping them from Casey's palm, brushing the girl's skin with her muzzle. As they stood together, a peaceful bubble enveloped them. In that instant Casey had no difficulty seeing through the mare's confident veneer to the vulnerable horse inside. Compassion welled up in her.

'You don't have to worry, girl. I'm going to take very

good care of you, I promise.' She rubbed Roxy behind her ears. For once the mare didn't sidle away as if Casey's touch was somehow repellent to her.

'Seen Morag, Case?' boomed Renata, leaning over the stable door. Infamously clumsy, she managed to kick over a bucket while she was at it. 'The vet needs to speak to her about the wormer she ordered and I can't find her anywhere.'

Roxy's ears flattened and she wheeled away from Casey as if she'd been struck.

Casey glared at Renata. 'If you could avoid scaring my horse half to death, that would be really helpful.'

The stable girl laughed. 'Oh, she's *your* horse now, is she? Thought she was on loan. Don't think the feeling's mutual. If you ask me, she doesn't seem too keen on you. Can't imagine why. Righto, if you see Morag, let her know I'm looking for her.'

As her footsteps faded, Casey tried to win Roxy round with another couple of mints, but the special moment had passed and they seemed once more to be on opposite sides of a wall. Not exactly adversaries, but hardly friends.

Casey thought about Salperton Park, less than three days away, and a knot formed in her stomach. There was a time not so long ago when she could have competed there invisibly. Now the eyes of the equestrian world were on her. Camera lenses sought her out. Sponsors held meetings about her. Fans expected miracles from her. Failure was a luxury she could no longer afford.

5

CASEY WAS NOT a fan of the 3 a.m. starts that were an inescapable part of eventing and tended to grumble and grouse as she yawned her way out of the bedroom. But once she'd splashed cold water on her face and downed a strong coffee, she was in her element. Rain or shine, there were few things she enjoyed more than preparing a horse to compete at its best.

It helped that Mrs Smith was a former dressage champion. Decades had gone by since she'd finished runner-up in the European Championships, but in the years she'd worked with Casey she'd impressed upon her pupil the importance of borrowing tips from the best dressage grooms. Casey had come to see her own pre-event ritual as part military operation, part art. Part science too because, as Mrs Smith often pointed out, a horse that isn't already in great condition is not magically going to look fabulous on the day. Good nutrition was critical to good looks.

For a horse who was borderline phobic about being touched, Roxy had proved surprisingly amenable to being made to look her best. She did not have the same objections to grooming or plaiting as she did to being tacked up, seeming actually to enjoy them, so Casey was able to work her way through an extensive to-do list with only a small nip for her troubles.

She liked to start the day with her own grooming routine. Before anything else, she wrapped the mare's tail in a damp bandage and ran a curry comb over her before backcombing the hair with a soft towel to remove any traces of dander. After using a soft brush on Roxy's face, legs and body, she trimmed the whiskers on her muzzle and under her chin. Mrs Smith had taught her to dab baby oil on the delicate skin around a horse's muzzle and eyes for added sheen. A polish with a dustcloth lent a burnished glow to the mare's coppery brown flanks.

Outside, the yard was still, the stars hidden beneath a blanket of overnight cloud. Wary of being kicked, Casey approached Roxy's tail with caution. Once the bandage was removed she used her fingers, not a comb, to untangle knots from the black hair.

'Nothing worse than a horse with a threadbare tail,' Mrs Smith always said. 'If every time you comb their tail they lose a few hairs, that adds up.'

Plaiting was an art in itself and one Mrs Smith had insisted that Casey master. She'd done so eventually, but only after much trial and error. Now she never went anywhere without her plaiting kit, which included brown, grey and chestnut elastics, waxed thread, large dull-tipped yard needles, scissors, a small metal mane comb, a seam ripper, hair gel and spray.

Once the last plait had been knotted to her teacher's satisfaction, Casey turned her attention to Roxy's feet, picking, washing and brushing them before applying dressing to the sole and wall of each. Finally, she cleaned and dried the mare's pasterns and the underneath of her fetlocks, an area prone to nicks and cuts. Some grooms liked to apply fly spray or show sheen to the body as a finishing touch, but Casey and Mrs Smith assiduously avoided any product that might inhibit sweating. As far as they were concerned, perspiration was an essential cooling mechanism for the horse.

By 4 a.m., Roxy was gleaming like a show pony. All that remained was for Casey to shower and pack everything she needed into the Jeep Wrangler they'd borrowed from Morag. Mrs Smith's elderly car was no longer up to the task of pulling the horsebox. Into the back of the Jeep went Casey's dressage and show-jumping jackets, three pairs of boots and breeches, two hats and four shirts. Saddles, bridles, rugs, bandages and eventing grease followed. The spare stall of the horsebox became a storage locker for horse feed, hay and bottled water.

Mrs Smith tapped her watch sternly as Casey scrambled to fill their ringside bag. It was a holdall that Mrs Smith liked to have on standby while Casey was warming up, in case of any last minute emergencies. Today, it contained a hoof pick, body brush, Polo mints, rain gear, a towel, a bottle of water, a couple of rags and a little pot of Vaseline, which Mrs Smith liked to rub on the bridle shortly before Casey's start time to make the silver bits gleam.

To keep Casey's energy up during the day, Mrs Smith also insisted that they pack a cooler box with protein drinks, homemade honey and oat bars and a lunchbox containing a quinoa, rocket, avocado, tomato and feta salad. In a separate container were rye bread sandwiches made with honey and crunchy peanut butter, which could be eaten at any time for an extra boost.

It was another half an hour before they were done. Frazzled and full of nervous excitement, Casey made her first attempt to load Roxy. The mare strolled into the horsebox without blinking an eye.

'Are you sure we have the right horse?' asked Casey as she hopped in to the Jeep. 'Not that I'm complaining or anything.'

Mrs Smith shrugged. 'She's clever. Perhaps, like us, she enjoys the adrenalin rush of going to shows.'

Minutes later they were on their way to Salperton Park in Cheltenham, Gloucestershire. As they drove out of the yard, Casey caught sight of Storm craning over his stable door, ears flickering uncertainly. It was only then she realised that he was probably bewildered that she was going to an event without him. She'd stopped in to say good morning as Mrs Smith groomed him, but she wished she'd had longer to reassure him.

She blinked away a tear. Without her horse she felt a little lost. Storm was her safety blanket. When she performed well it was almost always due to his courage, his talent and the almost mystical connection between them. As much as she was looking forward to the challenge of competing on Roxy, she couldn't shake the feeling that they were heading into a perilous unknown.

Once they were on the open road, however, Casey's nerves settled. Dawn came and went, a pink seam in the quilt of clouds. She drank coffee and half-listened to a country music CD as Mrs Smith drove. Ordinarily, she would have used the time to mentally rehearse the day ahead, but her mind kept returning to the previous night when Peter had come to Peach Tree Cottage for dinner.

The evening had started well. Mrs Smith had made a delicious curry with coconut milk and Casey had cooked a relatively successful rhubarb crumble. Afterwards, Mrs Smith excused herself and went to bed and Casey and Peter relocated to the sofa. One thing led to another and soon they were kissing.

The temperature in the room rose and not just because of the balmy summer air drifting in through the open windows. Casey slid her hands under Peter's shirt. She was running them over the muscles in his broad back and thinking how safe she felt in his arms and how much she loved him when her phone beeped.

'Don't get that,' murmured Peter and he bent his head to kiss her again.

But already Casey was wriggling away. 'Have to. What if it's urgent? Could be the event organisers texting everyone to say that Salperton's been rained off.'

'The only danger of that happening is if they've had an overnight monsoon,' Peter said wryly as he moved away and straightened his shirt. 'A week ago, they were in a panic because they hadn't had rain in a month and the ground was like concrete.'

Casey reached for her phone and a message flashed up:

Thinking about you. KW

She almost dropped it.

'Secret admirer?' Peter asked teasingly.

Casey felt the same rush of guilt and dread she'd had when Kyle West's bicep had inadvertently brushed against her in the yard. 'Don't be silly.' She jumped to her feet. 'How about a hot chocolate?'

He laughed. 'Now I'm curious. Who's texting you at 10p.m.?'

'Does it matter? Don't you trust me?'

''Course I trust you.'

'That's good to know, because I trust you too.' Their fingers entwined as Peter followed her into the kitchen. 'But if you must know, it was Kyle West. You know, the coach.'

Peter retrieved his hand casually. 'I do know. He has quite a reputation, and not all of it's to do with his talent around horses. I didn't realise you knew him.'

'I don't. I mean, he had some business at White Oaks a couple of weeks ago and while he was here approached me about taking him on as a coach. It was a two-minute conversation.'

'He was here and you didn't mention it?'

'I didn't mention it because it wasn't important. What's the big deal? Anyhow, I told him that Mrs Smith is the only coach I'd ever want or need. I'm not sure why he's contacting me again. I guess he's not used to taking no for an answer.'

'I guess not.'

Peter said no more about it, but it seemed to Casey that he held her extra close when she kissed him goodnight. As she climbed the stairs to her room her heart did little bunny hops of joy. It was the most amazing feeling in the world to love and to be loved.

But when sleep descended, the face she saw in her dreams was Kyle's. It was his blue eyes that hypnotised her and his golden head that bent to kiss her.

She woke in the early hours of the morning, sweating and absurdly guilty. Weren't dreams supposed to reveal the hidden desires of the dreamer?

But no, that couldn't possibly be it because she didn't desire Kyle in any way, not professionally and not romantically. It was true that on his visit to White Oaks he'd intrigued her and there was no denying that he was attractive, but his text had put her off. The arrogance of the man was beyond belief.

A blast of cold air and car fumes jolted her back to the present. Mrs Smith had pulled in to a motorway service station and parked in a quiet corner so that they could have breakfast.

When Casey climbed back into the Jeep after checking on Roxy, Mrs Smith was stirring boiling water into a lunchbox full of oats. She put yoghurt and cinnamon on top and handed it to Casey with a quizzical glance. 'You've been a million miles away all morning. I might as well be driving alone. What's preoccupying you? Is everything all right with Peter?'

Casey opened a pot of natural yogurt and added it to the porridge. 'Peter's perfect. I have a lot on my mind, that's all.'

'The only thing you should have on your mind is this morning's dressage test.'

'That is what I'm thinking about. Well, that and other stuff. Oh, I forgot to tell you, this company that makes horseboxes for quite a few of the top riders – Equi-Flow – wants to give us a free lorry. It's brilliant. It has space for four horses and luxury accommodation. There's a posh shower and toilet and the side opens out so you have a living area during the day and a room with a double and sofa-bed at night. Plus it has about six storage lockers for tack and feed. It's super-cool.'

'It would be cool if it were that easy,' Mrs Smith said drily.

'Meaning what?'

'Meaning there's no such thing as a free lunch. For every sponsor you take on, there's a time commitment. Pretty soon you'll find yourself with barely a minute in the day to do the thing that made you worth endorsing in the first place.'

'It's not like that,' said Casey, annoyed. 'They don't want anything from me. Obviously, I'll mention Equi-Flow if I talk to any journalists or do any magazine shoots, but basically all they're asking is that the Badminton and Kentucky champion is seen to be using one of their lorries.'

'But you're not going to be using it. *We* are not going to use it. Equi-Flow approached me after you won Badminton and I told them thank you but no thank you. Frankly, I think they have quite a nerve contacting you behind my back.'

Casey couldn't believe her ears. 'Are you crazy? Of course we're going to accept the lorry. Why would we turn down a free luxury lorry when it means we'll be able to stop borrowing Morag's horsebox? You know how it wobbles.'

'It was good enough to get you to Badminton,' Mrs Smith reminded her. 'Like it or not, we're going to continue to use it because there are no strings attached and because the Burghley Horse Trials are less than four months away. Do well there and you'll be able to afford a decent lorry of your own – one that does not make you slave to a corporation.'

For a long minute they glared at each other.

'I don't want to wait till Burghley,' Casey said stubbornly. 'If I'm presented with an option that will make Storm or Roxy more comfortable and my life easier, why would I turn it down? Anyway, it's too late. I've already told them that we want it.'

Mrs Smith was incensed. 'Well, I'm your manager and I'm going to tell them again that we are absolutely not having their lorry – only this time I'll make my point more forcibly.'

'Don't you dare,' shouted Casey. 'You have no right to dictate to me what I should or shouldn't do. I've never signed any legal document giving you permission to run my life.'

As soon as the words were out of her mouth, Casey regretted them, but it was too late. They hung in the air like a speech bubble, hateful and cruel.

Mrs Smith went still. 'That's true. You haven't.'

'I'm sorry. That came out wrong.'

Casey felt sick. Ever since the two of them had bonded years earlier at the Tea Garden Café in the East End of London, where Casey was a teenage waitress and Mrs Smith was an enigmatic customer with a bohemian style that was all her own, Mrs Smith had been a shining light in Casey's life. Far more than a teacher, she'd been a friend, mother, psychologist, healer, personal trainer and font of wisdom on everything from reviving starving rescue horses to the finer points of Zen Buddhism.

And, yes, she'd also acted as Casey's manager, dealing with sponsors and setting Casey and Storm up at Peach Tree Cottage and White Oaks Equestrian Centre when they didn't have a penny to their name.

They'd never discussed a contract, because all the legal documents in England could never be as binding as the sacred bond of trust that had always formed the core of their relationship.

With a single sentence, that bond had been shattered.

Casey laid her hand on Mrs Smith's arm. 'I'm sorry. I didn't mean it. Of course you're my manager – and a million other wonderful things besides.'

But Mrs Smith didn't look round. She put the keys in the ignition and the engine shuddered to life.

'No, you're right. We've never had a signed agreement. Ironically, I've never pressed for one because I didn't want you to feel that I was trying to run your life. Perhaps that's just as well. We have a flexible arrangement that can be terminated at any time, and I think we should keep it that way. Who knows when one of us might fancy a change.'

6

THE FIRST PERSON Casey saw when she approached the warm-up area was Kyle West. He was wearing fawn breeches and a close-fitting blue jumper that hugged his finely muscled frame. It was hard to believe it wasn't calculated for effect. Yet there was something boyish and vulnerable in the way he swept his sun-streaked fringe from his eyes. He grinned at her as she reined in Roxy.

'Just the person I was thinking of. It's becoming a habit, you know – thinking about you.'

'Twenty-eight days,' Casey advised.

'What for?'

'That's how long it takes to make or break a habit. Twenty-eight days.'

He laughed. 'Are you honestly telling me that I haven't crossed your mind at least once since we met? Not even in your dreams?'

Casey's face grew hot. She leaned over the other side of Roxy and pretended to be checking a stirrup leather. 'I'm not telling you anything at all. I'm thinking about my horse and my test, nothing else.'

'Quite right too. If I was your teacher, I wouldn't have it any other way. Speaking of teachers, here comes yours. Mind introducing me?'

Perhaps it was just the washed-out light of the overcast day, but Mrs Smith's skin looked almost translucent as she walked up. She and Casey had barely spoken since the awful argument in the car. Casey had done her best to make up for what she'd said and Mrs Smith had been coolly professional, but they both knew that something had been broken.

Casey straightened in the saddle. 'Angelica Smith, meet Kyle West. Kyle, meet Mrs Smith. You two should have a lot in common so I'll leave you to it. I'm off to put Roxy through her paces.'

She glanced pleadingly at her teacher. 'Any last minute advice?'

'Plenty, but I'll stick to one simple tip. Roxy isn't Storm. Remember that and you'll be fine.'

As Casey rode away, Kyle turned to Mrs Smith. 'It's a pleasure to finally meet you. I've been curious about you for quite some time.'

Mrs Smith's gaze followed Casey. She gave no sign that she'd heard.

Kyle leaned nearer. 'I mean, as a teacher, you're in a dream situation. You have a pupil who is not yet eighteen and yet already she's breaking records that have stood since the sport was invented. With the right help, the world is her oyster.'

'And you're implying what exactly, Mr West?'

'I'm not implying anything. I'm only saying that Casey represents the future of eventing. Twenty-first-century riders need twenty-first-century solutions. Modern methods. Cutting-edge techniques.'

The wind was getting up and a gust came at them with unexpected force. Mrs Smith clutched at the paddock rail for support. The remaining colour drained from her face and she gave a little gasp.

Kyle frowned. 'Are you okay? Can I get you a chair?'

With immense effort, Mrs Smith recovered her poise. 'Whatever for?'

'So you can sit down. You seem ... faint or sick.'

'I'm perfectly well, Mr West. Never better. Would you like me to get you a trolley?'

'What for?'

'In case you need help with your enormous ego.'

He laughed. '*Touché.*'

Mrs Smith didn't smile. 'If you'll excuse me, I have work to do.'

As she moved away, a man took her place at Kyle's side. A childhood accident had left his face with a peculiarly mashed appearance, as if all the character had been pummelled out of it. Over the years, Ray Cook had learned that the best way to divert attention from his looks was to move, dress and talk in a way that allowed him to blend into the background. Being a nonentity had proved so useful that Ray had actively cultivated it. People could spend months with him and afterwards find themselves unable to describe him, other than to say that he was of medium height and build and had brown hair and eyes. They recalled that there was something odd about him but couldn't say exactly what.

Ray spoke seldom and when he did his voice was quiet and had no identifiable accent. 'I think you might have met your match in Mrs Smith.'

Kyle didn't turn his head. Anyone watching the pair from a distance would have assumed the men were strangers. 'Oh, please. If I thought I couldn't take on an old woman, I'd hang up my boots today.'

'Maybe you should. That old woman, as you so disrespectfully refer to her, has probably forgotten more about riding than you'll ever know.'

Kyle's eyes narrowed. He watched Casey practising her rein-back and noted that, despite the fact that a couple of former Olympians were warming up, a sizeable majority of watchers were glued to Casey's every move. Kyle wondered what Casey's opinion of him would be had she overheard the conversation he'd had with Ray on the way to Salperton Park earlier that morning.

Ray interrupted his thoughts. 'Come on, Kyle, let's not waste time winding each other up when we have business to attend to. Casey Blue is about to start the dressage and I don't want to miss it. After that, I'll buy you a coffee and we can figure out what to do next. Whether you like it or not, we need each other.'

Casey entered the dressage ring in a working trot and tracked to the right. In the lead-up to Kentucky a fitness trainer called Ethan Grange had taught her how to meditate prior to performing. Never had she been more grateful. Driving into Salperton Park, she'd been so stressed and upset about her row with Mrs Smith that she'd been tempted to withdraw from the competition. A five-minute meditation had helped enormously.

To her credit, Roxy had been as good as gold all morning. She seemed to thrive in a competition environment. Her enquiring mind enjoyed new challenges, faces and places. On the way to the collecting ring, she'd been on her toes like a dancer, spooking and feinting, but Casey had the impression that it was all for effect. Roxy wasn't nervous in the least. She was excited.

In Casey, those emotions were reversed. Part of her had imagined that after being tested at the highest level in CCI****four-star dressage, elementary dressage would be easy, but she'd reckoned without the difficulty of attempting it on a strong-willed young horse. During the four minute test, she found herself working overtime to contain the mare, especially when she changed the rein and circled right.

By some miracle Roxy halted and was immobile for two or three seconds, as required. She even agreed to a five step rein-back, albeit with ears flat. But as soon as she was given permission to transition from a trot to a canter, she expressed her glee by kicking up her heels and surging forward.

The judges were inscrutable in their cars, shielded from the buffeting wind. Casey could imagine them hunched over their scores, taking a dim view of her failure to deliver the 'balance, uniformity of bend and lengthening of stride and frame' called for on the test sheet.

Fretting over her mistakes, she forgot to think about her test. As she and Roxy drew to the close of a twenty metre circle, completed at a furious pace, her mind went blank. For the first time in her riding career, she had absolutely no idea what movement came next. Panic seized her. It occurred to her that when she rode Storm *he* remembered the tests better than she did. *He* anticipated her questions and was ready with the answers. They were one unit, working in sync. The problem with her and Roxy was that they didn't trust one another.

She stole a glance at Mrs Smith, who was beyond the

ropes, directly in her eyeline, but her teacher's expression was unreadable. Two more strides and a line of expectant faces came into view, one of which was Kyle's.

Casey thought: *This is going to be beyond humiliating.* Beneath her tweed jacket and yellow bib, she started to sweat.

Then Kyle did something or said something. Afterwards, Casey was never sure which. She only knew that he communicated the next move to her as surely as if he'd whispered it in her ear: *half circle right.* Casey remembered the rest herself. *Return to the track at E. Counter canter.*

A final transition to trot and it was over. Casey left the arena trembling as if she'd just done the cross-country.

Mrs Smith took Roxy's reins as Casey swung out of the saddle. 'You lost concentration because you were thinking about Storm, weren't you?'

'Yes,' Casey admitted. 'I was. I can't help it. I miss him.'

She took the packet of Polo mints from the ringside bag and offered a couple to Roxy.

'It could have been worse,' Mrs Smith said flatly. 'It could have been better too, but it wasn't a total disaster. Put it out of your mind. You barely have time to change before the show jumping.'

It was only as she led the mare back to the lorry park that Casey dared to glance over at the place where Kyle had been standing. The young coach was no longer there. The only person remaining was a man dressed in beige who was staring at her rather intently. Casey smiled at him but he didn't smile back.

She turned away and promptly forgot all about him.

7

I T WAS THE poorest excuse for a summer's day in
memory and yet Salperton Park still managed to look
idyllic. Every corner of the estate was lovingly tended and
it showed. There were new roofs on the village houses,
gardens bursting with flowers, and the rolling landscape
through which the cross-country course threaded had
the timeless loveliness of an impressionist painting. The
house itself dated back to the seventeenth century and
provided an imposing backdrop for the show jumping.

Casey's start time was 9.45 a.m., but that was delayed
when a girl on an overwrought thoroughbred fell and
fractured her arm in three places. During her extended
warm-up, Casey had counselled herself very sternly to
stop comparing Roxy with Storm. It was both pointless

and unfair. Roxy's personality might leave a lot to be desired, but she was a first-class horse in her own right. It wasn't her fault if Casey lacked the experience to deal with her.

During the break Mrs Smith, who was obviously hurt by Casey's outburst in the car but making an effort not to show it, said something that stopped Casey in her tracks.

'Imagine it was Roxy who you rescued from the knacker's yard, not Storm. If that was the case, you wouldn't be getting frustrated with her. Nor would you be dwelling on her vices. You'd be the way you were with him – infinitely tender and patient. You'd know that she's a product of her past and it's up to you to understand her, not the other way around.'

These words stayed with Casey as she warmed up for the show jumping, shivering as the temperature plummeted to an unseasonal low and the wind strengthened. She tried not to be intimidated by the fact that Andrew Nicholson, one of the world's greatest riders, was sharing the collecting ring with her, along with an aggressive man with thinning hair and a large bottom who kept putting up the practice jump above class height, in violation of etiquette, as if they were competing in the Puissance at Olympia.

Casey shut him out of her mind and did her best to communicate kind thoughts to Roxy. Gradually, she felt the mare settle and calm. A key tenet in Mrs Smith's teaching was the importance of visualisation to success. Casey tried picturing threads of light bonding her and Roxy. She saw them flying over every jump and collecting a shiny trophy at the end of the day.

To a degree it worked. By comparison with those at four-star events like Badminton, the jumps seemed almost toy-like. But the whipping wind had brought a misty rain and it made for a challenging ride.

Roxy pulled hard, eager to take every fence at a gallop. As she soared over an upright flanked by two giant parrots, clearing it with air to spare, Casey had an insight into the untapped potential of the mare. She jumped with energy and confidence and she jumped cleanly. She was in her element.

They were unlucky to have one pole down, but Casey could not have been more pleased. She stood in her stirrups as Roxy cantered over the finish line, patting the mare and waving to her cheering fans. She hoped that Kyle was watching. It would be good to have him witness her putting in a decent performance.

That was her last thought before Roxy did her trademark sideways shy. It happened so suddenly and violently that Casey hadn't a hope of remaining in the saddle. She landed flat on her back, unable to do anything other than wheeze. There were groans of sympathy from the crowd.

Casey felt a surge of resentment towards the mare. She thought: *Why am I even surprised? She hates me. Her sole aim in life is to embarrass me.*

Kyle's concerned face loomed above her. 'Have you

broken something or are you just winded? Blink once if you have a serious injury or twice if the only thing wounded is your pride.'

Since sinking into the ground wasn't an option, Casey blinked twice. Kyle waved away the St John's ambulance crew who were rushing over with a stretcher. Without consulting her, he lifted Casey into his arms and carried her from the arena.

'I kind of like it when you're winded,' he remarked with a grin. 'It means you can't protest or come out with ridiculous lines about twenty-eight days. I can assure you that if you actually were to become a habit, it would take me a lot longer than that to get over you. What's that? Oh, you want me to put you down. Well, if you insist, but don't do it on my account.'

Casey was scarlet when he finally set her on the ground and not just because of her fall. She was in love with Peter but her body betrayed her whenever Kyle came anywhere near her. Being pressed against his chest, close enough to breathe in his sexy boy smell, had sent her blood pressure through the roof.

'Thank you for helping, but you shouldn't have done that,' she said, scowling to hide her confusion.

He laughed. 'Oh, but I did. You were holding up Andrew Nicholson.'

Suddenly shy, Casey looked away. 'You must be wondering how I've ever managed to win a single event. Every time you see me I'm either falling off or making an idiot of myself, or both.'

His blue eyes were twinkling. 'I'm not thinking anything other than it's a normal part of the process of adjusting to a new horse. My father says he's learned more from bad horses, or horses behaving badly, than he has from good horses.'

'So your dad's a horseman too? Does he teach?'

'My dad's dead,' Kyle said curtly. 'Sometimes I forget and use the present tense.'

Casey was mortified. 'I'm so sorry. I—'

'Don't be. He went a long time ago. I miss him, but I've made my peace with it. It is the way it is.' His smile was sad. 'Anyway, we were talking about you. I was about to say that you should look at the positives. Lady Roxanne has a pretty amazing jump on her. I'd like her in my yard. She has a couple of personality issues, but we could iron those out very easily.'

'And how would you do that?'

'Casey! There you are. What happened?'

Mrs Smith hurried up to them, wet and flustered, with bright spots of make-up on her cheeks. Tendrils of her silvery fair hair had pulled loose from their ponytail mooring and her multi-coloured Tibetan jacket contrasted bizarrely with Kyle's immaculate blue jumper and pale breeches. She paused to get her breath.

'Laura Collett's groom brought Roxy to me. She said you'd taken a tumble and been carried out of the arena. I had visions of you being carted away in an ambulance. Thank goodness you're okay. I'm afraid I missed seeing

61

you jump because I was in the bathroom. With the delay, I got confused about your starting time.'

Casey was annoyed. 'You were in the bathroom?'

'Yes, I was. Is that a crime?'

'No, it's not, but it would have been helpful if you'd seen Roxy's performance and could give me some advice. That's why you're here, isn't it? Kyle was just telling me that he believes she has a couple of psychological issues which could easily be resolved.'

Kyle lifted his hands in mock surrender. 'Hey, don't put me in the middle of this. I was only venturing an opinion.'

Mrs Smith regarded him coolly. 'I bet you were.'

Kyle shook his head as if he couldn't understand why she was being so petty. 'Casey, if you're feeling all right, I'm going to head to the members' tent for a quick bite to eat. I don't suppose you'd like to join me?'

'We have a quinoa salad waiting in the car,' Mrs Smith interjected.

'I've had a fall,' Casey said sarcastically. 'I think I need something a bit more substantial than a quinoa salad. Kyle, I'd love to join you if that's okay. I'll take care of Roxy and be right there.'

If Mrs Smith was offended, she didn't show it. 'Don't worry about it. It's all in hand. I'll look after Roxy. You kids enjoy yourself. See you in good time for the cross-country, Casey. If it happens, that is. According to the forecast, a storm is moving in.'

Back at the horsebox, Mrs Smith tended to Roxy before tipping both salads into the bin. Under normal circumstances she couldn't stand waste, but her stomach heaved at the thought of food. After allowing Roxy to munch some grass for a few minutes, she returned the mare to the horsebox. To her relief, Roxy boxed easily. But when she went to move away, the mare whickered softly. Mrs Smith smiled a weary smile. She pressed her cool cheek to Roxy's warm silken one and for a long moment the pair drew comfort from one another.

'Don't tell Casey how well we get on,' Mrs Smith said softly. 'She might take it personally.'

Unable to stay upright for another second, she sank to the floor in the other stall and lay stretched out in the semi-darkness, a wet cloth covering her eyes.

No matter how much she tried to distract herself, she ceaselessly returned to the same thought. What preoccupied her wasn't Casey, Kyle or even the cross-country. It was the two remaining Nurofen in the pocket of her Tibetan coat. She wanted them with the desperation of an addict, but she knew she needed to hold off until shortly before the drive home. If she didn't get the pain under control before she sat behind the wheel, she could put them all in a ditch.

Mrs Smith had lied to Casey when she claimed she'd got confused about her start time. She'd known to the minute when her pupil would be jumping. But shortly before Casey entered the arena, Mrs Smith had been swamped by an avalanche of agony so horrific it had sent her rushing to a Portaloo to throw up. When she emerged, she'd been so white and shaky that she'd had to down a fizzy drink – normally anathema to her – in an attempt to raise her blood-sugar levels in a hurry. Catching sight of her reflection in the glass counter of the burger van, she'd been shocked to see how wan she looked. When Casey fell, Mrs Smith had been sitting in the Jeep repairing her make-up.

She'd always known there would be a day of reckoning, but she'd convinced herself it would be a long way off and certainly after the Burghley Horse Trials. Now, it seemed, it was not to be. Angelica Smith's devotion to Casey, Storm and Roxy was total, but the pain that crashed with hurricane force through her body had become so debilitating that it made it impossible for her to do her job. Worse still, it was making it difficult for Casey to do hers, and that Mrs Smith would not tolerate.

But the idea of being without Casey and horses, her reasons for breathing, was almost as excruciating as the cancer eating her up inside. And Mrs Smith was in no doubt that that was what it was: Cancer with a capital C.

Five or so months earlier, Mr Andrew Mutandwa, an oncologist, had sent her for a battery of tests. Even before she left his office, he'd been frank in confiding that he feared the worst. For that reason, she'd deliberately given him a false address to which to send the results.

When at last a hospital letter did reach her, it was two days before the start of the Badminton Horse Trials. She'd been faced with a stark choice. If she opened the letter, the news might be a death sentence. At the very least she would have to undergo a course of radiation and/or chemotherapy which would compel her to abandon the girl and horse she loved at the hour they needed her most. Either way, life as she knew it would be over.

But there was another option. She could burn the letter without reading it and hope that the whole thing would simply go away. Out of sight, out of mind. So that's what she chose and in doing so incinerated her only chance of stopping the monster in its tracks.

Her promise to herself was that she would quit as Casey's teacher after Badminton and return to the hospital. But when Casey won the championship, she was immediately invited to compete in the Kentucky Three-Day Event. At that stage, Mrs Smith's pain was still manageable and there was a more pressing issue than her health. Casey and her father had become the victims of a vicious blackmail plot and once again Mrs Smith was needed. Then Casey won in Kentucky too and suddenly the Grand Slam was in play. And here they were.

And all this time Casey had no idea that she'd taken on a terminally ill coach.

Mrs Smith had hoped to keep the truth from Casey until after Burghley, in three months' time, but her encounter with Kyle West had changed everything. It was what he'd said about Casey being the future of eventing and needing 'modern methods' and 'cutting-edge techniques' that had really got her. With a few blithe sentences, he'd reduced Mrs Smith to the status of an ancient relic. Listening to him, she became conscious that her clothes were wrong, her teaching was wrong, *she* was wrong. If he'd stabbed her in the heart, he could not have wounded her more. She felt as if the lifeblood was leaking from her body.

Footsteps sounded outside the horsebox. Mrs Smith sucked in a breath, whipped the rag from her eyes and hauled herself to her feet. 'In here, Casey,' she called. 'I was about to grease Roxy's legs.'

Her brief rest had eased the pain enough that she could make a good show of tacking up Roxy for the cross-country while Casey changed into a red and white polo-shirt, air jacket and clean breeches. Lunch with the handsome Kyle seemed to have cheered her up considerably and she was clearly making an effort to be nice after her biting comments of earlier.

'Just enjoy yourself,' Mrs Smith counselled as they headed to the start of the cross-country. 'You and Roxy are still getting to know one another. Salperton is a lovely galloping track with lots of big, bold fences. It goes without saying that they don't have the degree of difficulty of those at Badminton or Kentucky, but Mike Etherington-Smith is one of the best cross-country course designers in the world so don't make the mistake of underestimating them. Give Roxy room to breathe and let her stretch her legs.'

She squinted at the seething black clouds overhead. In the distance thunder growled. 'Let's hope the storm holds off until you're done.'

As it happened, the weather was irrelevant. Roxy ran out twice at the second fence, the incongruously named Savage Selection Tasting Table, incurring forty penalties. Casey retired her at once.

Every rider suffered run-outs. Even veteran jockeys like Pippa Funnell and Zara Phillips lost championships because their horses baulked unexpectedly at obstacles, but that didn't lessen Casey's frustration.

As she hosed Roxy down and Mrs Smith used loading the Jeep and horsebox as a cover for swallowing her painkillers, the entire lorry park came to a collective halt. In through the gate came a lorry so vast and shiny that it cut through the gloom of the afternoon to dazzle all who gazed upon it. It was painted in blue and silver and emblazoned in scarlet lettering: EQUI-FLOW, PROUD SPONSORS OF CASEY BLUE AND STORM WARNING, WINNERS OF THE BADMINTON HORSE TRIALS & KENTUCKY THREE-DAY EVENT.

The pain in Mrs Smith's head and abdomen increased exponentially the closer the lorry came. Two photographers appeared out of nowhere and took pictures of its arrival.

'Tell me you didn't authorise this,' she said to Casey.

A broad grin spread across her pupil's face as she

secured Roxy's lead rope to the old horsebox. 'I'm afraid I did and I don't regret it one bit. Isn't it gorgeous? Isn't it the coolest lorry you ever saw? It's easily as smart as William Fox-Pitt's. It might not be as big, but it's perfect for Storm, Roxy and I. And you, of course. Come on, even you have to admit that it's fab.'

Before Mrs Smith could summon a response, the lorry braked beside them, closely followed by a Land Rover the size of a tank. The Land Rover disgorged an ebullient man with a pleased red face and spiky grey hair, two blondes in ludicrously high heels who looked like swimwear models, and a further two men wearing gaily coloured T-shirts and expensive suits.

'Casey Blue, what an honour to meet you!' cried the first man. 'Allow me to introduce myself. Edward Lashley-Jones at your service. Ed to my friends. I hear that you've had a bit of a disaster in the cross-country, but no matter. You'll be back to your winning ways very soon, I'm sure, and in the meantime it's fantastic that you're here to greet us and take part in the photo shoot.'

He gestured in the direction of his companions. 'Allow me to introduce my business partners, Rupert Pinkney and Tony Hampton and their ... partners, Candi and Mandy. Girls, would you like to show Casey around her new home, as it were?'

'Great to meet you all,' said Casey excitedly. 'Thank you so much for doing this, Mr Lashley-Jones – Ed. I'm over the moon. Can I introduce you to my coach, Angelica Smith?'

Ed Lashley-Jones' eyes slid over Mrs Smith and dismissed her. 'Excellent, excellent. Now we need to get on if we're to get the pictures done before the rain moves in. All right, Casey? We must have a little something for Her Majesty's Press.'

Casey gave her teacher an imploring glance. 'Come on, Angelica, let's explore our magnificent new lorry.'

Mrs Smith stood firm. 'There's no way I'm getting in to that thing.'

Casey blanched. 'Would you excuse us a moment?' Steering Mrs Smith away, she whispered: 'What are you doing? Why are you trying to ruin this for me?'

Mrs Smith was in too much pain to be diplomatic. The Nurofen had yet to kick in. 'Casey, I'm telling you for the last time that you're making a mistake. These people will bleed you dry and use your bones for soup. They're parasites.'

'And you know that for certain, do you? You have a crystal ball? You're unbelievable. You've met them for all of two seconds and you've already judged and condemned them – something you're always telling me not to do. Well, I'm sorry, I'm doing this, whether you like it or not. It'll be good for me and even better for the horses. Who cares if I have to do the occasional photo shoot. I'll be travelling in the lap of luxury and all for free.'

Mrs Smith inhaled an agonising breath. It took every ounce of willpower she possessed to remain standing. 'Casey, I'm only saying these things because I care about you and don't like to see you being used. Believe me when I tell you that this lorry will come at a price. If you do this thing, you can do it on your own. It's me or the lorry.'

'Everything all right, Casey?' called Lashley-Jones. 'I think I just felt a spot of rain. We must get these photos done now. Heaven forbid the girls' hair gets messed up. We'll never hear the end of it.'

'Your choice,' Mrs Smith said again. 'Either the lorry goes or I do.'

Casey's mouth set in a mutinous line. 'You go, Angelica. I choose the lorry.'

8

YOU GO, ANGELICA. I choose the lorry.

Three days after the Salperton Park debacle, Casey sat in the passenger seat of the lorry in question, sipping a cappuccino made by the state-of-the-art coffee machine in the lorry galley and watching the Wiltshire countryside unfurl before her. A banner of blue sky lent the scene a fairytale quality.

She was thankful that Mr Farley, the driver assigned to her by Equi-Flow, was the silent type. His conversation had so far been limited to asking her which address he should programme into the sat nav. Mr Farley was not included in the Equi-Flow package. Already, she had been billed for his services.

'You understand that Equi-Flow can't possibly chip in

for a chauffeur?' Ed Lashley-Jones had told her. 'I mean, we're giving you a quarter of a million pound wagon. Don't get me wrong, we're delighted to do it and you'll be a superb ambassador for our company, but we have to draw the line somewhere.'

Personally, Casey would have preferred it if the line he'd drawn was on his own consumption of champagne in the members' tent on Saturday night at Salperton Park. But in the end a drunken sponsor was only one of the many horrors she'd had to endure that day, and paled beside the events that followed.

After she and Mrs Smith had argued in the lorry park, Casey had been forced to paste a smile on her face and act as if nothing would give her greater pleasure than to pose for an excruciating number of pictures in front of her flash new 'wagon', as Lashley-Jones insisted on referring to it. The impromptu photo shoot caused a certain amount of derision and merriment among the passing riders and grooms. It also attracted many more autograph hunters.

While Casey was being shown the interior of the lorry by Candi and Mandy, Mrs Smith had slipped away in the old horsebox, taking Roxy with her.

To save face, a furious Casey had had to pretend that had been the plan all along. Unluckily, she was then at the whim of Lashley-Jones, who was providing the driver who would take her back to White Oaks in the new lorry. He and his cohorts headed straight to the members' tent, where they proceeded to put away as many seafood platters and glasses of champagne as they could manage. The only thing that saved Casey's sanity during the long evening that followed was thinking about Kyle, who'd come to her rescue for the third time that day, during the afternoon photo shoot.

Just as Rupert Pinkney was suggesting that she change into a tight-fitting Equi-Flow T-shirt and perch on the bonnet of the Land Rover with Candi and Mandy, the storm that had been threatening all day descended. In two minutes Casey was drenched to the skin. Abandoned by the Equi-Flow tribe, she was rushing for shelter when Kyle appeared out of nowhere with an umbrella. They took refuge in an officials' cabin, empty but not yet locked.

Kyle glanced at the goose bumps on Casey's arms.

'You're freezing, Casey Blue. Is it compulsory to suffer when you're doing fashion shoots or would you like me to escort you to your car before you catch pneumonia? This wind is absolutely wicked.' He squinted into the deluge. 'Where is the horsebox, anyway? Or have you already moved everything into the new one?'

Casey was shivering uncontrollably. 'It's gone. Mrs Smith's taken Roxy home. We ... we had words.' To her embarrassment a tear rolled down her cheek.

Unexpectedly, Kyle hugged her. 'I'm sorry.' He didn't probe. 'I'm guessing that you don't have a change of clothes?'

'I'm f-fine.'

'You're about a million miles from fine. Unfortunately,

I haven't brought any spare clothes with me, but you're welcome to my jumper.'

Ignoring her protests, he unzipped his brown leather jacket and pulled off the blue jumper that she'd admired earlier in the day. Beneath it was a white vest that emphasised every contour of his flat stomach, narrow hips and slim, strong arms. Casey's eyes dropped to his breeches and worn, mud-splattered boots. He was quite devastatingly attractive.

She swallowed. 'I have a boyfriend.'

Kyle's face was unreadable. 'This is not about whether you have a boyfriend or I have a girlfriend. This is about stopping you from catching your death of cold. If your boyfriend was here, I'm sure he'd be doing the same thing for you.'

He handed her his jumper. 'It was clean when I put it on this morning, but I can't vouch for it now. If you're willing to take your chances, it'll keep you warm till you can find something better. Keep the umbrella too. I think I have another in the car.'

He shrugged into his jacket and moved to the door. His gaze met and held hers. 'See you down the road, Casey Blue.'

Since her only other option was hypothermia, Casey stripped off her soaking polo-shirt and put on the jumper as soon as he was out of sight. It was still warm and smelled faintly of cologne and clean sweat. The soft cashmere enveloped her in a hug. As much as she tried to tell herself that it was a practical solution to the damp clothes problem and that anyone would have done the same, wearing it felt like a betrayal of Peter.

And for the rest of the evening she had to sit in the members' tent and listen to the merry chatter and inane questions of the Equi-Flow bunch, while the jumper clung to her like a second skin.

It was midnight when Casey finally crawled into bed at Peach Tree Cottage. Despite her exhaustion, she tossed and turned. Shortly before six, she gave up on sleep and crossed the fields to the stables. Roxy seemed disappointed to see her, which was good for neither her ego nor her spirits. As she opened the stable door, the mare looked past her hopefully as if she were expecting Mrs Smith.

'Just me, I'm afraid,' Casey told her with a sigh, wondering, for the thousandth time, what she had to do to win Roxy's approval.

She wondered too how she was going to win back Mrs Smith's. She felt ill about the things she'd said. They played in her head like a stuck record. Passing her teacher's bedroom door a little while earlier, she'd debated whether to take her a cup of chai and a bunch of wildflowers as a peace offering. She planned to apologise and promise to make an appointment with a lawyer that very week to have a contract drawn up making Mrs

Smith her official manager. Waiting for the kettle to boil, however, she'd decided that Mrs Smith might be in a more receptive mood if she'd had a decent night's sleep and some breakfast. With that in mind, Casey decided to deal with the horses first.

Peter turned up as she finished grooming Storm. He'd spent the previous day and night in Norfolk, shoeing Arabians for Lord Lavington. Casey, who was in the midst of a flashback featuring Kyle in his white vest, nearly had a heart attack. To compensate, she kissed Peter with a little too much enthusiasm. He laughed.

'I was worried about telling you what I'm about to tell you, but if this is the effect that my absence has on you maybe it won't be so bad.'

'Not planning to leave me, are you?' Casey asked with a smile.

'Leave you? You must be joking. You're the best thing that's ever happened to me. But I may have to go away for a while.'

He drummed his fingers on the stable door. 'Case, I don't know how to tell you this ... '

'You're making me nervous, Peter. Just say it, whatever it is.'

'All right, I will. Last night I had a phone call from the manager of the Lone Pine stud near Mount Juliet in Ireland. You've heard of Alejandro Hall?'

Casey had. He was the Argentinian farrier whose wizardry with the feet of horses had been directly or indirectly responsible for some of the greatest horse-racing triumphs of all time. It was said that he could take a donkey with laminitis and, after only three treatments, make it run like Nijinsky.

'I've dreamed of taking one of his courses for years, but he only selects a handful of people and the waiting lists are a mile long. I put my name down for one before I ever met you but until last night I'd never had a response.'

'And now you have?'

He looked sheepish. 'Now I have. There's an eleventh-hour cancellation. Only trouble is, the course starts tomorrow.'

Casey looped her arms round his waist. 'And that's a problem why? Surely that's the good thing about having a dad who's a farrier too? Evan can take over some of your work.'

'Yes, he can. It's not work that I'm anxious about; it's you, Casey. I don't like it when we're apart.'

'I know that, and I feel the same way. But this is the opportunity of a lifetime, Peter, and it's important. It's also your passion. You've gone to the ends of the earth to support me and help me pursue my dream. I'd be the most selfish girl ever if I didn't do the same for you.'

Peter's shoulders sagged with relief. He put his arms around her, letting his fingers find the hollow at the base of her spine, hot and damp after her efforts with the horses. 'Thank you. That means everything. I promise I'll call, text and email so often that you'll be totally sick of me.'

Casey ran a hand over the fine stubble on his jaw. Peter would never turn heads the way that Kyle did, but to her he was gorgeous and the kindest, most wonderful boy she'd ever met. That he also had the sort of body that adorned the cover of men's health magazines didn't hurt either.

She kissed him again. 'I love you.'

Conscious that it had taken her far too long to say it in the year before they got together, she now said it as often as she could.

He grinned. 'I love you too. You really don't mind that I'll be out of the country for ten weeks?'

'*Ten weeks?*' Casey pulled away from him. 'You didn't say anything about ten weeks. I thought you meant that you'd be gone five or six days. The Burghley Horse Trials will be starting by the time you come back.'

She wanted to scream, 'You can't go. I need you. Without you at my side every step of the way, I'll never win Burghley.' But she couldn't, for all the reasons she'd already said. Over the past few months, Peter had constantly put her career first, regardless of his own feelings. There was no way that she was going to deny him this chance.

Instead she took his warm hands between hers. 'What I meant to say is that the best thing you could possibly do is go away for a few months. You'll be spared all of my usual pre-event stress and angst and be back in time to use your newfound knowledge to fit Storm with the perfect shoes to help him with the Grand Slam.

It couldn't be better. I'll miss you like crazy, but I'll be happy knowing that you're doing something that makes you happy.'

'Really? Well, since you put it like that.' A smile spread like sunshine across his tanned face. 'Oh, Case, I'm so excited. I've wanted to meet Alejandro Hall for years. I—'

Footsteps rang on the cobbles. 'Hey, Casey, you've made page five of the *Daily Mail* today,' cried Renata, arriving at the stable like a small tornado, brandishing the newspaper. 'Boy, are you going to be breaking some hearts ... Ah, sorry, didn't realise you had company. Hi, Peter. Never mind, I'll pop back later.'

Peter reached for the paper. 'Don't be daft, Renata. Give it to me. If Casey gets hold of it first she'll decide she looks terrible and I'll never see it.'

'Okay, but don't shoot the messenger.' She beat a hasty retreat.

Peter opened the paper and went stiff. Casey had to bite back a squeak of horror.

Beneath the headline, FEELIN' KINDA BLUE, was a photograph of Kyle carrying Casey from the ring at Salperton Park. Casey's eyes were closed and her face was nestled into Kyle's shoulder. He was wearing the blue jumper that was presently tucked from view beneath Casey's pillow in her bedroom. To anyone unfamiliar with the situation, they looked like lovers in an intimate embrace.

TOP EQUESTRIAN COACH KYLE WEST, 20, COMFORTS 17-YEAR-OLD CHAMPION EVENTER CASEY BLUE, AFTER A FALL AT THE SALPERTON PARK HORSE TRIALS YESTERDAY. A SOURCE CLOSE TO THE PAIR INSISTED THAT THEY ARE 'JUST GOOD FRIENDS'.

Peter said quietly: 'Is there something you'd like to tell me, Casey?'

'No,' cried Casey. She snatched the newspaper and tossed it over the stable door. 'I mean, yes, there is something I'd like to tell you. It's not what it looks like. I had a fall. I was winded. While I was on the ground trying to breathe, Kyle scooped me up and carried me out of the ring because we were holding up Andrew Nicholson. That's it. That's all there is to say. Typical tabloid to read something more into it.'

Peter's arms were folded defensively across his chest. 'But why him? When he texted you the other night, you told me you barely knew him.'

'I don't. We've had two or three brief conversations and that's it. But what was I supposed to do? I was in pain and couldn't breathe. He kindly came to my rescue because he thought the first-aid people were taking too long to reach me. I'm afraid I was incapable of gasping, "Put me down! My boyfriend wouldn't approve."'

'Okay, okay, it wasn't your fault, but you have to admit that it looks bad. The whole country is going to think that you and Kyle West are an item. It's the last thing

I need to see when I'm about to go away for months on end.'

So don't go, Casey wanted to say. *Stay here and protect me from Kyle.*

What she needed protection from she wasn't sure. Perhaps herself. She felt guilty even for having the blue jumper. It was as if a little piece of Kyle was hidden in her bedroom.

She put her arms around him. 'Peter, I'm sorry about the photo. If the positions were reversed I'd be mad too. But it's you I love. That's all you need to know.'

His dark eyes bored into hers, seeking reassurance. 'I believe you. I also trust you. Don't ever think I don't. But you're famous now, Case. Look at your new lorry. Everyone will want a piece of you. People are going to be throwing money and temptation at you all the time. It's not always going to be easy to resist.'

He left soon afterwards. His plan was to drive home to Wales to collect a few things he needed for his course before flying directly to Dublin from Cardiff. He and Casey had walked arm in arm to the car park, smiling again and teasing one another, but both knew that the incident with Kyle West had cast a shadow over things.

Returning to the stables, Casey bumped into Morag.

'Nice wheels,' she said, nodding towards Casey's new lorry. 'Fit for a queen. Lot to live up to, but I'm sure you'll learn to deal with the pressure, especially if Kyle West has taken a shine to you. It's a shame that it's all got a bit much for Mrs Smith. I saw her climbing into a taxi last night with two suitcases.'

Casey's blood turned to ice.

Morag was watching her closely for a reaction. 'Bit of an odd time to take a holiday, isn't it, with only months to go till Burghley and Storm about to come back into work?'

Casey found her voice. 'Mrs Smith has not had a break for as long as I've known her. I'm not about to begrudge her a little time off. Now if you'll excuse me, I have a million things to do.'

As soon as she reached the field gate, she broke into a run. Her limbs felt weak. All she could think was, please God, let this be some terrible mistake.

She flew into Peach Tree Cottage and up the stairs. Mrs Smith's bedroom door was still shut. Casey paused, lungs burning. She wanted to hold on to the last moment when things were still the same. She wanted to believe that Mrs Smith was having a lie-in – perhaps reading *The Tao of Love* or a biography of the Dalai Lama. Casey would say sorry and give her a hug and they'd laugh about how silly it was to fall out over a lorry. They'd have breakfast together and plan the day.

There was no reply when she knocked. Inside, Mrs Smith's room was spotlessly clean, the bed stripped. Not a trace of her remained.

On the bed was a note. Casey's knees gave way and she sank onto the mattress. The paper shook in her hand.

Dearest Casey,

*Please don't blame yourself for my going. To be honest,
it's been a long time coming. Loath as I am to admit it, I'm
not getting any younger and things that used to be effortless
for me are now a struggle. Yesterday, things came to a head.
It wasn't so much because of our disagreement, although
I admit I was hurt. Rather it was because I came to the
reluctant conclusion that I can do no more for you. You're a
beautiful, talented young woman and I could not be more
proud of you, but you represent the future of equestrianism,
the 21st century, and I am about the past. You need a
dynamic young teacher who can take you to the next level.
You need modern coaching and cutting-edge techniques.
Mine would only hold you back.*

*One of your many wonderful traits is that you are loyal
to a fault. You'd never end our relationship, even if you
agreed with any of the above. For that reason, I think it best
to leave now, before you come home. Our time together has
been the most precious of my life and I'm proud to have
played a part in helping you to flourish and grow. In return
I ask only one favour of you. Don't try to find me. Focus
on your own life and on your preparation for Burghley. Be
happy. Above all, be true to yourself.*

Your loving friend always,
Angelica Smith

For what seemed like hours, Casey sat in the echoing silence, too heartbroken to cry. She was roused from her misery by her phone buzzing in the pocket of her jeans. The call was from an unknown number. She prayed it was Mrs Smith.

'Casey, it's Kyle.'

'Oh.'

'I can't imagine what I've done to generate such enthusiasm,' came the dry response. 'Unless you're cross with me about the photo in the *Daily Mail*. Personally, I rather like it. It's already pinned on my office wall … Joke. That was a joke.'

'Kyle, what do you want?'

'Want? I don't *want* anything. When I last caught a glimpse of you, you were being dragged in the direction of the champagne tent by the Equi-Flow piranhas. I'm only calling to check that you made it home safely and that you're feeling okay after your fall. I also wanted to tell you that you rode much better than your results, if that's any consolation.'

Casey pulled herself together. 'I'm sorry. I didn't mean to be rude. Thank you so much for the loan of your jumper. It was a lifesaver. Unfortunately, something awful has happened.'

It all came out then. The arguments with Mrs Smith. The devastating note.

Kyle listened without a word. Finally he said, 'Would you like me to help you find her? I know a man who knows a man who might be able to track her down.'

'NO!' Realising that she sounded slightly hysterical, Casey took a deep breath. 'Thanks, Kyle, but no thanks. If Mrs Smith doesn't want to be found, the least I can do is respect her wishes. Anyway, she's better off without me.'

'Maybe *you're* better off without her.'

'That isn't true. Mrs Smith is the best person I've ever known. I've always needed her far more than she's needed me. Everything I've ever achieved is because of her. I depend on her utterly. I don't know what I'm going to do. I'll be lost without her.'

'Casey, you've achieved the things you have because of your talent, passion and hard work, not because of Angelica Smith. I'm not denying she's a good teacher, but don't underestimate your own ability – or Storm's.'

'Thanks, but—'

'Casey, I know this situation is hard for you, but I don't want you to worry about a thing. I'm going to take care of you.'

'You have reached your destination!' chirruped the sat nav, startling Casey from her reverie. 'You have reached your destination!'

'Blasted machine,' barked Mr Farley, speaking for the first time in two hours. 'Always says we've arrived when we obviously haven't. Don't see no horses around here.'

They'd come to a halt in a shadowed lane overhung by the intertwined branches of oak, sweet chestnut and yew. On the left side of the road an overgrown track wound through the trees and out of sight. Craning out of the window, Casey spotted a faded wooden sign obscured by the vines and purple flowers of a deadly nightshade plant: Rycliffe Manor.

'I thought your Mr West had one of the best yards in the country,' grumbled the driver. 'The entrance doesn't look promising.'

Casey, who was thinking much the same thing, said primly: 'He's not *my* Mr West.'

They bumped up the track, grass brushing the underside of the lorry. Casey grew increasingly nervous. Perhaps they should turn back before it was too late. She could always say she'd changed her mind.

'Mr Farley ... ' she began.

The lorry gave a final, defiant surge and burst from the trees. Sunlight flooded into the cab. Stretching before them were three hundred rolling acres of exquisitely pretty parkland. A manor house, partially obscured by a high hedge and trees, looked grandly on, while a smart granite signpost directed visitors to the Rycliffe Manor Equestrian Centre along an immaculately graded gravel road.

'This is more like it,' said Mr Farley as they passed white-fenced paddocks in which sleek, glossy horses nibbled at waving emerald grasses. 'Now what were you saying?'

'Nothing.'

Casey gripped the edge of her seat, palms sweaty. As they neared the stables, she saw a girl with short auburn hair lunging a chestnut horse. Sparks of sunshine bounced off his hide. Beyond them was a field of professionally designed show jumps. It could have passed muster at Hickstead.

In the car park, Casey climbed stiffly from the lorry. She inhaled deeply. The air was fragrant with the mingled smells of horses, wood shavings and jasmine. As she approached an iron gate set in an archway, Kyle appeared on the other side. His face lit up at the sight of her. Hurrying forward, he slid open the bolt and let her in. 'Welcome to Rycliffe Manor, Casey. I'm so glad you could make it.'

'It's good to be here.'

'Great. Let's show Roxy her new quarters and then I'll give you a quick tour.'

As she led the mare to a light, airy stable in a block made of creamy Cotswold stone, Casey had to stop herself from gasping out loud. It was simply the most stunning training facility she'd ever seen. The stables themselves lined two sides of a manicured grass courtyard, in the centre of which was a tinkling fountain. Roses bloomed in beds of blazing colour.

An indoor school flanked the third side of the courtyard and signposted paths at each corner led to a horse therapy pool, two ménages and a cross-country course. Order and cleanliness reigned. Not a wisp of hay was out of place.

Kyle was watching Casey's expression. 'Do you approve?'

'Approve? I love it. It's magnificent.'

Kyle grinned. 'See, I told you I was going to take care of you.'

9

THE FIRST SHOCK to Casey's system was Kyle's teaching style. Whereas Mrs Smith's approach was heartfelt, spiritual and intuitive and as likely to involve scraps of wisdom she'd gleaned from *The Way of the Peaceful Warrior* as it was techniques picked up when she was a dressage champion, Kyle was all business.

'I have one hard and fast rule,' he told Casey as he led her to what he called his 'video suite' above his office. 'I never discuss training or give advice outside a lesson. Don't ask me because I won't respond. The way I see it, you wouldn't go to a doctor or a lawyer on the street and expect them to give you free medical or legal advice. Why is a riding expert any different? It's no problem if you want me to work with you at an event, but it needs to be organised in advance.'

He smiled. 'Fair enough?'

'Of course,' Casey said hastily, thinking about Mrs Smith, who'd been happy to discuss technique and plan strategy twenty-four seven and who couldn't have cared less about money. Casey had paid her ten per cent of her winnings and, since her victory at Badminton, taken over the rent payments at Peach Tree Cottage. But that was nothing compared to the fortune Mrs Smith had secretly spent supporting her in the early days of their relationship. Casey had tried to pay her back, but Mrs Smith claimed to have lost all the receipts.

Kyle ushered Casey into a small room filled from desk to ceiling with the latest computer and audiovisual equipment. As they entered, a man stood up quickly. His thinning hair and the sallow skin of his strange, squashed face were more or less the same uniform beige as his chinos and polo-shirt.

'Casey, let me introduce you to Ray Cook, my right-hand man,' said Kyle, patting him affectionately on the back. What Ray doesn't know about horses isn't worth knowing and the whole place would go up in smoke if he left. Ray, I'm sure Casey Blue needs no introduction. Badminton and Kentucky Three-Day Event champion. One of the most talented young riders in the country. I've asked that she give us forty-eight hours to prove to her that we're worthy of helping her win Burghley, so we all have to be on our best behaviour.'

Ray smirked but made no response.

'Pleased to meet you,' Casey said. He looked familiar but she couldn't place him.

Ray shook her proffered hand and left the room with nothing but a muttered, 'Great. Well, I'll be off then.'

Kyle shrugged. 'As you can tell, I don't employ him for his personality.'

They sat down at an oak bench weighed down by an X-box, a professional video camera, a couple of computers, a television and two banks of monitors showing CCTV footage of the indoor and outdoor schools, the cross-country course and a couple of roads on the estate.

Kyle pulled over a laptop. Three videos were cued up on it. He hit play on the first. It was Casey's dressage test at Salperton Park. She watched herself battle to contain Roxy as the mare kicked up her heels before plunging into an energetic and uneven canter, ears flattening when she was asked to transition into a trot.

Next came the show jumping. Casey squirmed in her chair as she watched herself fly from the saddle when Roxy shied. The part where Kyle carried her from the ring in his arms had, mercifully, been edited out. The third video showed Roxy run out at the second fence in the cross-country.

Kyle pushed back his chair. His polo-shirt, breeches and long boots were all black, which somehow emphasised his golden skin and hair. Casey thanked her lucky stars that he was being so business-like. It didn't lessen his attraction but it did help keep her mind on the task at hand.

'Looking at those, what do you feel went wrong?'

'Everything,' Casey said at once.

'Not at all. You did most things right. Your problem is one of concentration. Each time you lose focus, Roxy senses that and reacts badly. Watch again.'

As the video played, Casey saw immediately that he was right. Here was the moment when she thought about Storm. Here was when she relaxed and allowed her mind to drift to Kyle and Peter. Here was when she thought about fence three when she should have been thinking about fence two.

'Come,' Kyle said, 'let's go and visit Roxy.'

On the way downstairs they passed Ray, who was returning to the video suite. Casey smiled at him, but he looked past her as if he hadn't noticed.

Roxy was munching hay in her spacious stable. Her ears went back when they appeared at the door and she made no move to come over to them.

Kyle took what looked like earplugs from his pocket. 'Hearing aid,' he explained. 'I find it helps me when I teach. My pupils don't have to shout when they talk to me.'

Casey smiled. 'Makes sense to me.' She opened the stable door. 'You told me at Salperton Park that Roxy had a couple of issues, but that they could easily be fixed. What are they?'

Kyle leaned against a pillar. 'I'll begin with a question.

I've no doubt that you've worked incredibly hard on getting to know Roxy and trying to make her feel comfortable, but have you found that she's continued to be a menace? Is she prone to biting, kicking, bucking or shying, mostly for no apparent reason?'

Casey was amazed. 'Are you psychic? That's exactly how she's been.'

'What was Mrs Smith's advice?'

'She told me to be infinitely patient and said that horses like Roxy are like Japanese Puzzle Boxes. As soon as you solve one question, you're presented with another.'

Kyle laughed. 'That's one way of putting it. Another is to understand that in Roxy you have a horse with huge potential but one who is as intelligent as she is insecure. Her "vices", for want of a better word, come out of boredom or fear. That's why she responded so badly when you lost concentration at Salperton Park. She's so sensitive to your mood that she felt abandoned. Deal with these factors and you'll have a champion.'

'Great. How do I do that?'

'It starts right here. She needs to spend as little time as possible in the stable during the day. When she is inside, I'm going to have Ray pipe classical music and BBC Radio into her stall so she feels she has company. We'll also give her a specially designed hay net that requires the horse to use ingenuity in order to get at the food. But in the summer I'd prefer her to spend most of her time outdoors where she has lots of natural stimuli to keep her amused.'

'What about training?' Casey asked. 'How do I keep her entertained or feeling supported when I'm working with her?'

'You have to keep finding new challenges and make her use her brain. With a horse like this, I'd advise keeping lateral work to a minimum. Work on a few specifics, make a big fuss of her when she gets something right, then take her out for a hack or a cross-country gallop. How long have you had her on loan?'

'Nearly a month.'

'Good. So you've had plenty of time to bond with her. Go over to her and give her some attention.'

Reluctantly, Casey approached the mare and rubbed her neck. Roxy's only response was to show the whites of her eyes and stamp a foot.

'When you show her affection, does she normally respond in a hostile way?'

Casey was forced to admit that she did on most days. 'Although she's better at events.'

'So it's safe to say that you've failed to bond with her? Then that's our number one priority. Until the two of you connect, she's not going to do her best for you. In fact, she's going to expend most of her energy trying to hurt you or get one over on you. The problem is, we don't have a lot of time. We'll need to come up with something pretty dramatic if we want to change her response quickly.'

94

He grinned. 'Don't look so crestfallen. We'll get there. And when we've sorted out Roxy, we'll move on to Storm.' He glanced at his watch. 'It's lunchtime. Let's grab a sandwich and coffee. I want to talk to you about your riding.'

Casey crawled into bed that night. It was a wonderful bed, a snowy expanse of Egyptian cotton sheets and duck down, which was especially welcome because she felt as if she'd been beaten all over with a baseball bat.

Kyle's first lesson had been entirely abstract. No physical riding was involved. Over lunch he'd informed her that her biggest weakness was her lack of experience with other horses and that it was critical that she addressed it. He presented her with a list of ten horses. She was to spend an hour working with each during the two days she was at Rycliffe Manor.

'Would you like me to work on anything in particular?' she had asked and was told to use her imagination.

Midway through the meal, a helicopter landed noisily in the field outside. Kyle dashed off to give a wealthy client a lesson. As instructed, Casey spent forty minutes schooling Roxy on her own before turning the mare out into a field. For the remainder of the afternoon she rode, in succession, a 17hh piebald cob with a sluggish stride, two jumpy ex-racehorses and a black gelding who pulled like a train. By 6 p.m., her arms were in such pain she could barely lift her fork to her mouth at the dinner table.

It was strange, and strangely thrilling, to be going to sleep in such close proximity to Kyle. His double-storey house, constructed from the same honey-coloured stone as the stables, was only a stone's throw from the equestrian centre's guest quarters.

Lying in bed, Casey checked her phone apprehensively. One message was from her dad, who was very excited to have been whisked to Florence at short notice on a cloth-buying mission with Ravi Singh. Two messages were from Peter – one to say that he'd landed safely in Dublin and missed her already, and a longer one raving about the breathtaking landscape of the Lone Pine Stud in Mount Juliet, where he'd be spending the next couple of months.

He added a P.S. *Hope you've had a good time at Rycliffe Manor. Do what's best for you, babe, and don't worry about anything else. Pxx*

Casey texted him an account of her day with lots of kisses on the end and pressed send. She felt much better. Before he left Wales, she'd called him with the news about Mrs Smith going. Peter had been stunned. He adored her teacher and found it difficult to comprehend that she would walk out on Casey with the Grand Slam in sight purely on the basis of a couple of heated exchanges.

The trickiest part of the conversation had been

breaking it to him that she was thinking of taking on Kyle West as a coach. There'd been a series of muffled curses. Finally, he'd come back on the line. 'Why him, Casey?'

And she'd had to attempt to explain that she didn't have time to shop around for coaches – not with Roxy being impossible and Storm about to return to full training. Kyle was one of the best. If he was keen to take her on, she had to go with him. Apart from anything else, she had obligations to her sponsors.

To his credit, Peter had been great about it once he'd had a chance to digest the news. 'I understand why you're doing it, but that doesn't mean I have to like it. I'd even go so far as to say that Kyle might do a better job than Mrs Smith. I'd just prefer it if the bastard wasn't so good-looking.'

Propped up in the pillows, Casey flipped through the latest issue of *New Equestrian* magazine, which had a cover story on Kyle. She too would have preferred it if he was less attractive, but wishing it wasn't going to change one hair on his head. Thank goodness he was so professional around the yard. It was only when he'd escorted her to her room that she'd caught a glimpse of his customary charm.

'Sorry it's been a bit mad around here today. I haven't been able to give you as much attention as I'd have liked. I did ask Ray to keep an eye on you and he was impressed. That takes some doing, I can assure you. Said you handled the racehorses like a pro.'

Casey had taken the opportunity to return his washed and folded jumper. Kyle took it from her with a rueful smile. 'I was hoping you'd keep it. I liked the thought of you wearing it.'

Casey had been so flustered that she'd practically shoved him out the door. Kyle was dangerous. No matter how much she tried to fight it, he got under her skin.

Judging from the article, she was not alone. The journalist called it the 'West effect'.

What everyone would like to know is how a high-school dropout whose only contact with horses was the beach donkeys in his seaside hometown became guru to the stars before he was out of his teens. The answer is elusive. West is the definitive International Man of Mystery. Even his former riding teacher is bemused.

'Kyle went from being the boy most likely to fail his BHS Senior Equitation and Coaching certificate to getting a distinction and wowing everyone who knew him,' said Terry Bond. 'It was as if suddenly, overnight almost, he was brushed with angel dust. I'm proud of him. He has everyone from Saudi princesses to former Olympians queuing for a sprinkling of that Kyle magic and I'm delighted to have helped him along the way.'

Part of the reason for West's meteoric rise is his state-of-the-art equestrian centre at the sumptuous Rycliffe Manor, home to multimillionaire Steve Remington. Before they fell out Remington was a business associate of Lionel Bing, father of West's former star pupil, the now disgraced Anna Sparks ...

At this, Casey stopped reading in shock. Anna Sparks had once been her most bitter rival. In the years leading up to Casey's Badminton win, vain, beautiful and prodigiously gifted Anna had reigned supreme as the best young rider on the eventing circuit. Along the way, she'd made it her mission to humiliate Casey and poke fun at her East End background and cheap clothes at every turn.

When, in spite of everything, Casey rose through the ranks, Anna tried to snatch Storm away from her and destroy her chances. But her maniacal obsession with winning at all costs backfired spectacularly. In a karmic twist, she was banned from eventing for five years for whipping a horse at Badminton. Millions of television viewers witnessed the horrific incident. No one had seen or heard from Anna since. There were rumours that she'd moved to Dorset to live with her mother, a music teacher.

Casey flung down the magazine, feeling ill. Kyle had coached her sworn enemy. There was no way that she could take lessons from a man who'd had anything to do with Anna Sparks. He must have known she was hideous. Casey glanced at her watch. She should pack her suitcase and leave immediately.

But how? Mr Farley had gone for the night. The chances of her getting a cab to collect her at 10 p.m. and drive her from the wilds of Wiltshire all the way to Kent were slim at best. Plus it would be astronomically expensive.

Distraught, she picked up the magazine. She might as well hear what Kyle had to say in his own defence.

What she read next changed everything. Kyle, it turned out, had almost had his fledging career destroyed by the fallout over Anna Sparks.

'It's human nature,' West says now. 'People always want someone to blame. With Anna out of the picture, it was me. That's okay. I understand that. But it hurt my clients, cost me business. Some felt tainted by association. It was painful because I love horses and it sickened me that people might think I in any way sanctioned that kind of behaviour. Anna disappointed me just like she did a lot of other people.'

Before he could recover, fate struck another blow. Philippa Temple, head of the Equestrian Centre at Rycliffe Manor, who'd taken West on as assistant manager after he finished runner-up in the Golden Horseshoe Riding Instructor Awards, was killed in a freak car accident. The brakes failed as she drove home alone from a show. A devastated West almost gave up on teaching altogether, but was persuaded by friends and clients to continue.

'I felt I owed it to her,' he says.

Casey slumped into the pillows. She'd read about Philippa's death at the time, but never having heard of her before hadn't really taken it in. Poor Kyle. That explained the little boy lost look that sometimes sneaked through his confident, sophisticated exterior. He'd been through hell. Well, she for one was not about to desert him. He'd condemned Anna Sparks' actions. That was good enough for Casey.

She turned off the light and lay in the darkness listening to the night creatures. Sleep descended so suddenly that it caught her in mid-thought, but it was a sleep plagued by dreams in which Mrs Smith was at the wheel of a runaway car. Over and over Casey tried to save her in the new lorry. Over and over she failed.

10

THE HAPPIEST ROBIN in the world woke Casey at the crack of dawn. As a shaft of orange sunlight slanted across her pillow, she dragged herself upright. Her muscles still ached from the previous day, but she wasn't tempted to go back to sleep. On the bedside table was the list of horse names given to her by Kyle. Her task today was to 'work on something different with every one'.

Walking stiffly to the stables a little while later, Casey wondered if a massage counted – for her, that is, not the horses.

Fortunately her first ride of the day was an easy one. Poetic was a twelve-year-old brown mare with a sweet, kind temperament. She was eager to please and much loved by her owner, a young girl. Casey did some light dressage work with her and was quite sorry to return her to her groom. She pined for Storm.

Looking in on Roxy, she found that the mare had already been fed and groomed and was leaning contentedly over her door while Taylor Swift sang country songs to her. She ignored Casey, as usual, but seemed cheerful enough.

'We tried her with Mozart and Beethoven, but she didn't take to them at all,' said the auburn-haired girl Casey had seen lunging the chestnut.

'Can't say I blame her,' Casey responded with a laugh. 'A lot of classical music stresses me out. I'd choose Dolly Parton over Wagner any day. I do like Bach though. My coach sometimes plays *St Matthew's Passion* on the way to events and it's amazingly soothing.'

The girl frowned. 'I didn't know that Kyle was into classical music.'

Casey's face grew hot. 'I meant my old coach – I mean, my last coach, Mrs Smith. Umm, I'm Casey Blue.'

'We all know who you are,' the girl said drily but not unkindly. She shook Casey's hand. 'Hannah. I'm a junior instructor here. Apologies, I thought it was a done deal, you and Kyle. Professionally, not romantically, I mean.' She giggled. 'I hear you have a boyfriend, which is nice. Peter Rhys, is it? Storm's farrier?'

'Uh, yes,' responded Casey, bemused by this segue.

'Anyway, Kyle likes you as a rider, you know. You're all we've heard about for weeks. Casey this and Casey that.

Ray approved of how you handled the thoroughbreds yesterday and believe me, it takes a lot to impress Ray.'

'That's what Kyle told me. What's he like?'

'Ray's all right. A man of few words but he's pleasant enough and he knows how to run a business. Kyle's a genius at what he does so it's best for him not to be distracted with the boring day-to-day things. Ray keeps the centre ticking over nicely and that works for everyone.'

She glanced at her watch. 'Please tell me that's not the time. I was supposed to meet someone in the indoor school ten minutes ago.'

After breakfast and a hair-raising attempt at the show-jumping course on a highly strung Arabian the colour of whipped cream, Casey went in search of Kyle. He'd been rushing about all morning, but he'd promised to analyse some video footage of her riding Roxy and a couple of other horses.

Kyle had told her to meet him in the video studio at ten, but Casey was early. Unable to control Adonis, the Arab, and fearful of falling off or injuring one of the most valuable horses in the yard, Casey had returned him to his stable after just thirty minutes. As a result, it was 9.48 a.m. when she reached the office building. Halfway up the stairs she heard raised voices.

'No!' yelled Kyle. 'No, no, no. It's too risky. It's the craziest thing I've ever heard and I don't want anything to do with it.'

'That's because your emotions are involved,' Ray said silkily. 'It's business, pure and simple. It's about what works.'

'The way it worked with Mouse, you mean?'

There was a silence. 'I thought we agreed not to talk about that again. That wasn't my fault. The girl was out of control.'

'Yes and on this occasion so are you, Ray,' snapped Kyle. 'What if something goes wrong? Do you really want that on your conscience? Try anything and you and I are going to have a serious problem.'

A floorboard creaked. Casey darted into the bathroom on the landing. She flushed the toilet and ran the water in the basin, emerging in time to see a scowling Ray going by. She smiled and was astonished when he quickly wiped the cloud from his face and smiled back.

'Morning, Casey. How did you get on with Adonis?'

'He, h-he's a handful,' stammered Casey.

'Yes, he is, but we're working our magic on him. In a month's time he'll be a different beast.'

With that, he was gone. Shaking her head in puzzlement, Casey went up to the video studio. Kyle was bent over his iPad, playing a video game where he hacked angrily at bits of fruit with a machete.

'Sorry,' he said when he saw her. 'Guilty secret.'

Casey pulled up a chair. 'Actually, it's quite endearing. You'd be too perfect otherwise.'

His hands stopped moving on the screen. A bleak look flitted across his face. 'Casey, if you knew me, you wouldn't say that.'

So suddenly that afterwards she wondered if she'd imagined everything that came before, he gathered himself and gave her one of his usual heart-melting smiles. 'Right, let's look at some of the footage from yesterday.'

There were three short videos – one of her working with Roxy and a couple of her riding the lazy cob and the first racehorse.

'We'll start with you and Roxy,' said Kyle.

Casey waited expectantly.

'So there you are. You're in the ménage with Roxy ... Looking good. We need to address some of the issues we talked about yesterday, but otherwise you're doing fine. Better than fine, in fact.'

'Which particular issues?'

'What I told you yesterday. Concentration and bonding and stuff. Let's take a look at these other videos. Here you are with Barnaby, the cob ... ' They stared at the video together. 'Great,' said Kyle. 'I wouldn't change a thing.'

He closed the lid of the laptop with a bang. 'What I'd like you to do this afternoon is take Roxy around the cross-country course. Stretch her legs and give her something to think about.'

He was up and out of the video room before Casey had time to ask another question, leaving her bemused and wondering whether Kyle blew hot and cold with all his pupils or if it was something unique to her.

By the time Casey had schooled three other horses and grabbed a sandwich for lunch, it was almost five o'clock. Her body was tired and ached all over, but it was perfect weather for a gallop: overcast and warm without being hot.

The cross-country course wound its way through the most glorious part of the estate. Roxy seemed to appreciate it as much as Casey did. Her head was up and she was relaxed but bouncy. Casey was tensed to hang on in case she shied at a fleeing rabbit or the blackbirds, finches and robins rustling in the hedgerows, but Roxy seemed fascinated by her new environment, not afraid. Her big lustrous eyes were popping out of her head.

As Casey let herself through the gate that opened onto the cross-country course, she had to pinch herself. Though small, the fences were close to Badminton quality, imaginatively designed and built by experts. If she signed Kyle's contract that evening, all of this would be hers – not literally, but it would mean that she could train here any time.

It helped allay the doubts that had crept into her mind

after the argument she'd overheard and the vague way in which Kyle had analysed the videos. Ray was an odd character and she could imagine him being difficult to deal with at times. Following their heated exchange, Kyle had obviously been in no mood for picking apart her riding faults. But one bad day didn't make him a bad teacher. Ninety-nine times out of a hundred he'd be the star coach everyone said he was.

With that final thought, she urged Roxy forward. The mare settled into a smooth gallop, clearing the first brush fence with room to spare. Balanced lightly in her stirrups as Roxy effortlessly negotiated flowerbeds, logs, oxers and even a mini water jump, Casey felt a surge of happiness that their working relationship was improving. It frustrated her that they were still business acquaintances rather than friends, but she supposed Mrs Smith was right. Bonding with a horse took time and patience. There were no shortcuts.

At the thought of Mrs Smith, Casey's stomach gave a lurch. She wished that there was a number she could call so that she could at least check if her teacher was all right. Quite apart from the guilt she felt over the awful things she'd said, she was plagued by fears that Mrs Smith had been hiding the true state of her health and could in fact be grievously ill. She might be sick, scared and alone and Casey would never know.

Tears blurred the next fence. Roxy lost impulsion and refused an easy post and rails. After circling back and coaxing the mare over it, Casey told herself off. Hadn't

Kyle told her that losing concentration was one of her biggest faults? She couldn't expect miracles from Roxy – or Kyle – if she didn't deliver as a rider. The buck stopped with her.

Roxy's performance, on the other hand, was exceptional. When they flew over the final fence, which was adjoined to the first, the mare was barely out of breath. Casey made a big fuss of her as they slowed to a walk.

She was about to dismount to open the gate when she noticed it was padlocked. This was problematic for two reasons. One, because she'd left her phone behind and couldn't call the equestrian centre for assistance, and two because Hannah had expressly told her that on no account should she use the only other gate, which was situated close to fence ten. 'Two crazy horse-hating dogs live along that lane and trust me, you do not want to run into them.'

For that reason, Casey spent twenty minutes leading an increasingly agitated Roxy up and down the fenceline in the hope of spotting a passing worker or rider who might rescue them. She was sure that Kyle, Hannah or one of the grooms would notice that she'd been gone for ages and come in search of her. But apart from a faraway tractor and a distant speckling of sheep the landscape stayed depressingly empty.

In the end Casey had no choice but to try the other gate. Such was her desperation that she was profoundly grateful to find it unlocked. Before allowing Roxy to go through it, she listened carefully. The lane ahead appeared to be a peaceful avenue of mossy trees and musical birds. If any horse-hating dogs did pop out of the bushes, she made up her mind to do her best to keep Roxy to a walk and not to do anything to provoke them. If they did get aggressive, Roxy was fast enough to outpace them.

Nevertheless, her heart was in her mouth as she set out along the green tunnel. Once inside it the birdsong was muffled and the air smelled of rotting leaves and moist, fertile earth. Roxy's appreciation of the estate's flora and fauna evaporated as they proceeded. She spooked at every squirrel and leaf. Casey tried soothing her, but she was on edge herself and it didn't work.

'In ten minutes we'll be back and I'll be hosing you down and giving you a nice dinner,' she told Roxy. 'This will all seem like a bad dream.'

They drew level with a cottage hidden behind a high hedge. There was a sign on the white gate: *Beware of the Dogs. Enter at Own Risk.* Casey laid a nervous hand on Roxy's shoulder. 'Easy, girl. We're going to be just fine.'

Her ears strained for a bark or a growl, but her only warning was the clink of a chain. Like a vision from a nightmare, a Rottweiler and a Doberman Pinscher hurdled the gate and came at them on silent paws.

The Rottweiler attacked first, springing at Roxy's neck, only narrowly missing her jugular. The mare screamed in terror, rearing so high that she almost overbalanced. Somehow she righted herself and came crashing down, landing a glancing blow on the Doberman. With Casey clinging petrified to her neck, Roxy wheeled and bolted along a track cut through the trees.

Casey's one hope – that the dogs would lose interest when their territory was no longer under threat – was in vain. Their determination to hunt down their prey increased with every bound. The rough track didn't help. Roxy was galloping at breakneck speed, but the ground was pocked with rabbit holes and fallen branches and each step was a disaster waiting to happen.

We're going to die, thought Casey. *We're going to die or suffer a horrific accident and there's not a thing I can do to stop it.*

A five-barred gate appeared in front of them. Roxy hesitated, took two extra strides and then it was too late. She was too close to make the leap. As she came to a plunging stop, Casey saw that the dogs were almost upon them.

They were trapped.

Flinging herself to the ground, Casey snatched up a stick. Over her dead body would they hurt Roxy. She ran forward brandishing her weapon. 'Get away!' she screamed. 'Leave us alone!'

They paused, snarling. The Rottweiler charged first, retreating with a squeal as she landed a blow. The Doberman darted around her to try to get at the mare. Casey tried to strike it but missed. It sprang at Roxy's flank, drawing blood. The terrified mare cowered against the gate, neighing wildly.

Casey swung at the Rottweiler as it lumbered forward to join the game, and hit the Doberman a crack on the nose as it moved in to attack Roxy again. Enraged, the dogs now turned their attention to her. The Rottweiler sank its teeth into her boot, shocking Casey into dropping the stick. It gripped her ankle like a vice. She was defenceless as the Doberman, his pointed ears pricked and yellow fangs bared, crouched to spring.

A piercing whistle blasted through the trees. The dogs looked crestfallen. White-eyed and whining, they melted into the undergrowth.

Casey ran sobbing to Roxy. Taking careful hold of her bridle, she stroked the mare's quivering neck. 'I'm sorry. I'm sorry. I made a mistake and I could have got you killed. Oh, God, Roxy, I'm so sorry.'

She expected the mare to wrench away or try to bite her, but Roxy did none of those things. She buried her nose in Casey's shirt, hiding her eyes like a frightened child. Casey put her arms around her and held her close. The mare's coat was dripping with white foam and blood. How long they stood there she didn't know.

'You're okay, I take it?'

Girl and horse started violently. Ray was striding towards them.

'I-I think so.' Casey's voice shook. 'I'm not sure. Roxy's been bitten.'

Ray moved closer. 'It's a scratch. It'll heal in no time.' His dull brown eyes were lit with a strange fire. 'What are you doing here? You could have been killed. The dogs are not pets. They're guard dogs. I told Hannah to be sure to warn you not to use the second gate on the cross-country course. If she forgot, I'm going to fire her on the spot.'

'It's not her fault,' Casey said hastily. 'She did tell me not to use the gate *and* she warned me about the dogs.'

'Then why—?'

'Because the main gate was locked,' cried Casey, her voice rising as the full horror of the situation started to sink in. 'I didn't have my phone and I waited for ages in the hope that someone would come by. Nobody did so I decided to chance the lane. When she said that there were crazy dogs along this road, I didn't know she meant Cujo and the Hound of the Baskervilles. *What?* Why are you looking at me like that?'

'Because,' Ray said grimly, 'you and your horse nearly ended up as dog meat for nothing. You made a fatal error. The main gate doesn't lock. It's always open.'

'What are you talking about? I saw the padlock with my own eyes. It was a big brass one.'

But Ray was already striding down the track. 'Show me. We need to walk right past the gate on our way back to the stables. I'd like to see this phantom padlock. And don't worry, I've chained up the dogs.'

Casey was so furious at being disbelieved that she had to bite her lip to stop herself saying something she regretted. 'Fine. Lead the way.'

They were approaching the gate when Kyle came roaring up in a pickup truck. He was out of the vehicle

113

almost before it came to a halt. His face was full of panic.

'When they said you hadn't returned, I thought you might have had a fall. What happened? Are you okay? Why is Roxy bleeding?'

'Despite being explicitly warned not to do so, Casey took the back gate,' Ray told him. 'It's not her fault. She wasn't to know the dangers. I'm afraid the dogs—'

A look of naked fury flashed across Kyle's face. A vein pulsed frantically in his jaw. 'The *dogs*?'

'I'm sorry,' Casey said miserably. 'The main gate was locked. I couldn't get out. I was getting desperate.'

Kyle stared at her. 'But that gate is never locked. It hasn't been locked once in the eighteen months I've been here.'

'I'm sure Casey knows a locked gate when she sees one,' Ray said in the tone of someone who thought the opposite. 'Let's take a look.'

'At the phantom padlock, you mean?' jibed Casey, still smarting from his earlier remarks.

He had the grace to look ashamed. 'Apologies. I spoke rashly in the heat of the moment.'

With Roxy following so closely that her muzzle was in constant contact with Casey's arm, they walked over to investigate. When they reached the gate there was a long silence.

'But it was there,' Casey insisted. 'There was a brass padlock. It was glinting in the light. How could I have imagined something like that?'

Ray held up his hands as if he, too, was mystified. In

114

reality, he was probably thinking she was an idiot.

'Forget about it. No real harm's done. You handled yourself well. You put your horse first and she thanks you for it.'

Roxy was so intent on being close to Casey, she was practically leaning on her.

'Thank you for saving me, Ray,' said Casey, trying not to sound ungrateful. 'I hate to think what would have happened if you hadn't come along when you did.'

The fire had gone from Ray's eyes and they were once again veiled and dull. 'No problem. I hope it doesn't colour your view of Rycliffe Manor. It's usually pretty peaceful around here. '

With a nod to Kyle, he struck off across the fields without a backward glance.

Casey looked pleadingly at Kyle. 'The padlock was there, I promise. I'm not making this up.'

He put an arm around her shoulders and she could feel the heat of his skin through her shirt. 'I believe you, Casey, don't worry. I'll make some enquiries. I'm sure there's a simple explanation. Maybe one of the temporary estate staff mistook this paddock for one of the sheep fields. Try to put it out of your mind. The main thing is you're not injured. Now let's get Roxy to the stables. I'll walk with you and send someone back for my truck.'

Casey managed a weak smile. 'I'm fine, really. You go. I'll see you there.'

She tried to move away, but Kyle moved with her

and kept his arm around her. 'Are you kidding? On my watch, you and Roxy have been frightened half to death. I feel responsible. I'm not letting you out of my sight until I know you're safe and sound.'

11

CASEY SLEPT IN Roxy's stable at White Oaks for the next two nights. She'd called Morag on the way home to ask if there was any chance that the mare could move into the stable beside Storm's. Morag's approach to horses and training was the polar opposite of Casey's and they hadn't always seen eye to eye, but the stable manager had a big heart. Casey was only midway through recounting an edited version of the dog attack when Morag interrupted.

'Consider it done. Anything you need, hon, anything at all, I want you to call. Seriously, I mean it. Night or day, don't even hesitate. We're here for you.'

Casey was deeply touched. She clicked off her phone,

put her arms around Roxy and they stood like that all the way home.

When the lorry was finally parked in White Oaks' familiar driveway and Mr Farley was on his way to a local pub for the night, Casey unloaded Roxy and led her to her new stable. It was piled extra high with the best bedding and had a bucket of water and hay net already installed.

After settling the mare in, Casey nipped next door to say hello to Storm. He was ecstatic to see her and she clung to him as if he was a life raft in high seas. In a way, he was. For the moment, he was all that remained of her support team. There was no one else that she could talk to and nobody at all who she could ask for advice about Rycliffe Manor Equestrian Centre. Peter was too biased against Kyle, her father knew next to nothing about horses, and Morag would have made some cutting comment about 'celebrity teachers'.

But Storm always made her feel better. He was so intelligent and his love was so constant that just being around him reminded her that by saving him, she had done something right once. And on that day, she'd relied on her own judgement. She'd made a decision to rescue him, regardless of the consequences, and she'd changed both of their lives for ever. Casey sighed. She wished she could stay longer, but the purple twilight was turning black and she knew she had to prioritise Roxy.

Still traumatised, Roxy grew anxious when she was left alone for even a moment. Casey virtually sprinted across the fields to Peach Tree Cottage to fetch a sleeping bag, pillow and blanket. She'd barely been gone for forty-eight hours and already the air in the house smelled stale. Passing Mrs Smith's bedroom, she saw again the stripped bed and the coat hangers dangling forlornly in the empty cupboard.

Down in the kitchen it occurred to her that she hadn't eaten since lunchtime. But there was no bread for toast and the milk was sour. Mrs Smith usually ordered the groceries and she was gone. Dejected, Casey tried calling Peter but his phone went straight to voicemail. She wasn't in the mood to leave a message, nor did she want to think about where he might be or who he might be with. Desperate to hear a comforting voice, she rang her dad, but his phone was switched off. She supposed he was still in Italy. She was glad for him, but it added to her sense of isolation.

Roxy whickered a welcome when Casey returned and watched with interest as the sleeping bag was unrolled on the stable floor. Before turning in, Casey put another application of manuka honey on the small puncture wound on Roxy's flank. The mare barely flinched. She made no attempt to nip Casey or crush her against the wall, simply gazing at her with adoring eyes.

The thing that kept coming back to Casey was Kyle's comment about how they needed to come up with something dramatic to bond Roxy to her, and how quickly that had come to pass. She stopped the thought there. She didn't want to think about the padlock, glinting in the light. And she definitely didn't want to dwell on the dogs and their yellow killer eyes and snarling savagery and what would have happened if Ray hadn't arrived when he did – Ray who, it had turned out, was responsible for the feeding and training of the guard dogs.

Casey snuggled into her sleeping bag. At least she had two friends in the world – Storm and Roxy. Four if you counted Peter and her father, and five if you added Mrs Smith. Mrs Smith would be her friend always, she knew, but Casey had not been a very good friend to Mrs Smith. Not at all.

And what of Kyle? Was he a friend?

Either way, he was her new teacher. She'd signed the contract before leaving Rycliffe Manor that evening. The office secretary, a briskly efficient bottle-blonde named Joyce, had lent her a fountain pen to fill in her address and other details. As Casey scrawled her signature a bubble of ink had oozed from the nib and run down the page. It was blue ink, but for a split second Casey's brain had turned it red so that it resembled blood.

Tucked up in her sleeping bag, she was scared to shut her eyes in case the dogs returned in her nightmares. When at last she did drift off, she didn't have a single dream. Neither did Roxy. All night long, the mare watched over her, her delicate nostrils fluttering as she breathed in the scent of the girl who'd saved her.

Next morning Casey started riding Storm again. He was fat and full of beans after his long holiday, but it was heavenly to be riding him. Since all she planned to do was hack him across the fields at a walk or slow trot, she took Roxy along on a lead rope. Morag thought she was mad and said so, but it couldn't have gone better. Storm and Roxy had made eye contact over their stable doors and had taken a liking to each other. Before the end of the ride, they were firm friends.

At the beginning of July, Casey entered Roxy in the Westwood Classic in Winchester. So inseparable had the mare and Storm become that Casey was tempted to bring him along to keep them company, but she was reluctant to unsettle him. She wanted to ease him back into training and keep him relaxed and content for as long as possible before the pressure starting piling on.

The new lorry was the last word in luxury. Every surface had a mirror shine and the seats smelled of new leather. The galley kitchen had everything the champion rider could possibly need and the foldout bed was so comfortable it almost swallowed Casey when she tried it out. In the back, Roxy had room to spare.

But with only the taciturn Mr Farley to share it with, Casey found it hard to enjoy the lorry on her own. It was like being a child left alone in a giant toyshop. The best toys in the world were no fun if you had no one to play with.

Added to which, her sponsor, Ed Lashley-Jones, was already becoming insufferable and she was only weeks into her contract.

'Congratulations on appointing Kyle West as your coach,' he'd rung to say when the news broke. 'Smart move. Handsome young man at the top of his game. Much better for your image as eventing's youngest superstar than that Mrs Smith who—'

'Careful, Ed. I'd like to remind you that it was Mrs Smith's coaching that got me where I am.'

Perhaps sensing that he'd strayed into a danger zone, Lashley-Jones backtracked smoothly. 'Of course, of course. I only meant that West is the man of the moment and you couldn't have made a better choice.'

He hung up after reminding her to promote Equi-Flow to any reporter, sponsor or top rider she came across. 'But only if you do well. If you have a meltdown, the way you did at Salperton Park, it's best not to mention us.'

With that vote of confidence ringing in her ears, Casey arrived at the Westwood Classic. The lorry park was already humming with grooms checking plaits and doing last minute touch-ups and riders on their way to the collecting ring. Casey saw nobody she knew. She couldn't ever remember feeling so lonely at an event. Lots of people said hi or stopped to talk to her, but many were strangers or acquaintances keen to be associated with her only because of what she'd achieved. She did have lots of friends on the circuit, but they were all away or busy.

To distract herself, she took her time putting on white breeches, a smart tweed jacket from another new sponsor and highly polished brown boots. As always, the last thing she did before she rode was put her mum's rose brooch in her pocket, only now she kissed it first. In the absence of everyone else she loved, it was infinitely soothing to know that her mother at least was always there.

She also texted her father.

How's Italy, Dad? Hope u r having a fab time. Envious. Seems ages since we spoke. Would love you to come on the road with me some time. Miss you. Cxx

No sooner had she sat down than she was up again. Caffeine always made her restless. She'd breakfasted on a motorway-service-station croissant and three cappuccinos from the lorry's fancy coffee machine. It was the kind of breakfast Mrs Smith would have heartily disapproved of, but, Casey told herself defiantly, Mrs Smith wasn't here. Kyle was.

He came striding up as she swung into the saddle. Casey noticed right away that he had in his hearing aid. He was wearing his blue jumper again, this time with faded black jeans that hugged his hips.

'For luck,' he said with a grin, tugging at the jumper. His blonde fringe flopped endearingly across his face.

'I'm not sure about that,' said Casey wryly. 'When I last wore it I had to spend an evening in the champagne tent with Ed Lashley-Jones and Mindy and Cindi. Or was it Candy and Bambi?'

Kyle laughed. 'Look at it this way. You did survive. That's saying a lot. And this teacher is here to stay.'

'Speaking of which, do you have any advice? What should I think about in the dressage?'

'Actually, the thing I want you to think about is what you do *before* the dressage. I noticed at Salperton that your collecting-ring strategy leaves a bit to be desired. You want to make sure that you have Roxy's attention and that she's relaxed. Try a few transitions – trot to canter and vice versa – and then bring her back to a walk. Next time ask her for a halt. Keep her guessing.

'As for you, your main task is to stay in the moment. There's nothing you can do about a mistake you made thirty seconds ago. It's gone. What you can do is focus on making the following movement as flowing and beautiful as possible. Oh, and Casey ... '

'Yes?'

'Don't forget to have fun.'

12

COMPETING IN THE intense, electric atmosphere of Badminton and Kentucky had been the most exhilarating experience of Casey's life, but she'd forgotten how much she enjoyed the buzz of the smaller events. Eventing was a great equaliser. The rigorous qualifying system ensured that the giants of the sport had to bring their young mounts on alongside those of policemen, bricklayers and nurses riding every shape, breed and colour of horse.

At times it made for chaos in the lorry park and collecting ring, but the risk factor in horse trials meant that it attracted as many genial cowboys as it did women who were fazed by nothing. Most people took most things in their stride.

Despite her achievements, Casey always got an attack of butterflies before competing. More so today because she didn't have Mrs Smith standing on the sidelines with her ringside bag full of emergency items. Casey especially missed her homemade granola bars. The croissant had not been a good idea. It had left her feeling bloated and lacking in energy.

Kyle caught her eye and smiled reassuringly. Besieged by a steady stream of fans – pretty girls, potential sponsors and the relatives or partners of riders who wanted to know if the 'West effect' could boost their rankings, he dealt charmingly with each. But his focus never left Casey. He made her feel special.

Gradually, her nerves steadied. Roxy was keyed up but responsive and Casey entered the dressage arena feeling confident. She intended to do her best, but all that really mattered to her was that she and Roxy were a team. Day by day the bay mare was learning to trust and accept her, just as Storm had. That alone was like winning the lottery.

The previous week Casey had called Roxy's owner, Jennifer Stewart, and asked if she could buy the mare. After their ordeal at Rycliffe Manor and the relationship they'd built since, Casey already knew that she would not be able to bear parting with Roxy in two or three months' time. She also believed that Roxy was a star in the making and her price would soon shoot up. When that happened she'd quickly be out of Casey's price bracket – if she wasn't already.

But Jennifer Stewart was a canny bird. It turned out she was a lawyer. Casey had opened the conversation by apologising for their dire performance at Salperton Park. She'd hinted that Roxy might have personality issues. But Jennifer Stewart cut her off in mid-sentence with a breezy, 'Now that you're working with Kyle West, I'm anticipating a drastic improvement. It would be rash of me to part with the mare at this stage. As she moves up the rankings, she'll leap in value.'

Depressed, Casey had ended the call. She couldn't lose Roxy, had to find a way to keep her. For a minute, she'd contemplated riding badly on purpose for the next few events so that Jennifer Stewart would decide that the mare was a no-hoper and be glad to part with her, but she'd banished the thought almost immediately. It was selfish and wouldn't be fair to Roxy. Roxy had a talent. Casey would be letting both of them down if she didn't encourage the mare to shine.

And shine Roxy did. The finer points of dressage were still new to her, but she was razor sharp and learned quickly. She also had wonderful natural balance, a critical ingredient in a dressage horse. Those qualities, together with her newfound affection for Casey, helped her to an assured performance that morning.

It was sheer bad luck that mid-way through, Roxy spotted a Rottweiler panting behind the ropes. It was on a lead, but that made no difference. Before Casey could stop her, she'd bolted halfway across the dressage court.

It was a measure of how much they'd bonded that

Casey was able to pull her up within a few strides. Gently, she persuaded Roxy to continue. Bearing Kyle's words in mind, she put the incident behind her and focused on making the rest of the test perfect. Her heart was pounding, but she softened her hands and did everything she could to communicate calm to Roxy.

Kyle was quietly pleased.

'There's work to be done, especially on her quarters, but the change in you both is extraordinary. I'm still embarrassed about what happened at Rycliffe Manor. When I said that we needed to find a dramatic way of uniting the two of you, I didn't have a mauling by rabid dogs in mind. You'll be glad to hear that we're reviewing our safety measures. The second gate is now locked and chained so that nobody else will ever make the same mistake you did.'

Casey didn't want to think about the dogs ever again and said so. After that, she blocked them from her mind so effectively that she and Roxy managed a clear round in the show jumping with only two rattled poles.

She'd changed out of her show-jumping gear and was making herself and Kyle a cappuccino in the new lorry when she heard raised voices outside.

'I don't believe it,' Kyle was saying in an agitated tone. 'That's impossible. There must be some ghastly mistake.'

When Casey went out, he was talking to Sam Tide's girl groom, Marsha. He looked quite shaken.

'What's going on?'

Marsha hesitated but Kyle snapped: 'Oh, for goodness' sake, tell her. She'll find out soon enough.'

'Find out what?'

'Anna Sparks.' Marsha's small brown face twitched with righteous indignation. 'Your nemesis. You'll never believe it, but she's here. Right here at Westwood Park. It's disgusting.'

'I'm surprised that she's brazen enough to show her face at an event, but there's no law against it,' said Casey. 'Just because she's banned from competing, doesn't mean she can't watch. She'll be a pariah, though. No one will speak to her.'

Marsha was hopping with indignation. 'You don't understand. She's not watching, she's competing. The ban has been overturned on appeal. They're reporting on Sky news that she claimed that some pills she was taking – diet pills, would you believe – made her act irrationally and violently. She told the appeal panel that that was the reason she attacked Franz Mueller's poor horse at Badminton.'

Casey was stunned. 'And they believed her?'

'There'll be an outcry, but yes they did. You're not going to want to hear this, Case, but she's competing in the same Intermediate class as you. Like a villain in a soap opera, she's back. Anna Sparks is back.'

When Roxy burst from the D box in the cross-country a little while later, Casey had only one goal and that was to vanquish Anna Sparks. She rode like a girl possessed. Every hurt that Anna had ever inflicted, every slight and every time she'd ridiculed Casey for having ill-fitting charity-shop clothes, or the wrong tack, or horsebox, or a knacker's-yard horse added fuel to the fire of Casey's loathing.

But the thing that really drove her on was what Anna had done to Storm. After Lionel Bing, Anna's wealthy father, had tricked his way into stealing Storm (money had changed hands, but as far as Casey was concerned it was theft), Anna had attempted to ride him – with disastrous results. The injury he'd sustained at their yard had caused him a huge amount of suffering and nearly cost Casey her career. Yet evil Anna Sparks was back competing as if nothing had happened.

'Whatever it takes, you have to beat her today,' Kyle had told her grimly. 'I don't care if you finish fortieth and she finishes forty-second. I just want you to finish ahead of her.'

'Oh, I will. You can take it to the bank.'

Whether it was because the Rottweiler had stirred up memories of the attack at Rycliffe Manor, or purely because she picked up on Casey's recklessness and rather liked it, Roxy responded with everything she had. They flew around the cross-country course as if they were at Badminton. Fruit tables, skinnies, ditches and a water jump featuring real flamingos – Roxy took them all in her stride. Sometimes she leapt so high and so boldly that Casey, expecting a more modest jump, was almost unseated.

Once, she thought she saw Ray in the shade with a video camera, unsmiling and dressed to blend with the crowd, but when she glanced back there was no one there. She decided she must have imagined it. If his right-hand man was at the Westwood Classic, surely Kyle would have mentioned it.

The crowd at the event was tiny in comparison to that at Badminton or Kentucky, but their enthusiasm more than made up for it. The applause swelled as Casey rode. If Roxy hesitated, Casey urged her on with a passion that was almost manic. The finish line flashed by all too soon. Then it was over and Casey, still high on adrenalin, was out of the saddle and hugging Roxy. Roxy's legs were trembling with effort, but her ears were pricked and she looked as if she was smiling.

'Did we do it?' Casey demanded as Kyle came rushing up and threw his arms around her. 'Did we crush Anna Sparks?'

Kyle grinned. 'I told you this blue jumper was lucky. You annihilated her, baby! Not only that but I think you might have won. *We* might have won – Team West. There are two riders who could still get past you, but I have it on good authority that neither is particularly strong on the cross-country phase.'

He was right. Team West had won the Intermediate class. An overjoyed Casey collected her prize to great cheers.

When she returned to the lorry, she found to her astonishment that it was the most popular in the park. The living area had been extended, the mini bar was open and music was blaring. Kyle was serving drinks to an ebullient crowd, most of whom were strangers to Casey. There were wolf-whistles and more cheers when she walked up. Michael Edge, a former Badminton champion, came over to tell her how well she'd ridden. Lots of people asked for her autograph.

The phone rang constantly. First it was her dad, who she'd texted to report that she'd won. 'Casey, I'm so proud. I can't talk long because I'm in Italy – back tomorrow ... but what is this about you changing coaches? How could you possibly break it off with Mrs Smith?'

Annoyed that he immediately jumped to the conclusion that it was she who had done the leaving, Casey pretended she couldn't hear him and told him she'd call back when she had a chance.

Ed Lashley-Jones called next. 'Casey, you little beauty. I knew you had it in you. I wanted to remind you that you're obligated to mention Equi-Flow if you speak to any journalists. I don't want to put words in your mouth, but if you could say something to the effect of, "My Equi-Flow lorry, the best on the market, played a big part in my success today," I'd be most grateful.'

'Mr Lashley-Jones—' began Casey.

'It's Ed to you, Casey Blue. I also wanted to give you a nudge about looking in your diary to check your availability for a paintball contest and a polo outing. I did email but haven't heard back. As per your contract, we have a string of corporate days coming up. You'll be expected to entertain our clients, give lessons and pass on tips. Motivational speaking is what we want.'

Next it was Jackson Ryder from *New Equestrian* magazine. 'Congratulations, Casey. That's quite a turnaround from your performance on Lady Roxanne at Salperton Park. Has changing teachers had anything to do with it?'

Kyle came over with a glass of champagne. Casey almost never touched alcohol but she took it from him gratefully. A few sips of fizz and she felt invincible.

'Has changing teachers affected my performance? Absolutely. Kyle is a magician. For us to achieve what we have in a matter of weeks is phenomenal.'

'Best decision you ever made,' Kyle whispered in her ear.

'Best decision I ever made,' Casey told Jackson Ryder laughingly. As soon as the words left her mouth she wished she could take them back. After all Mrs Smith had done for her, how could she say such a thing? It was as if fame was going to her head just like the champagne.

'So you fancy your chances at the Burghley Horse Trials in two months' time?' Jackson Ryder asked.

Casey wanted to tell him not to print her previous

comment, but Kyle was so close she could almost feel his body heat and she didn't want to offend him. 'Burghley? I'm feeling great about it. Storm Warning is back in training. Provided he stays fit, we'll be going for the Grand Slam with everything we've got.'

'You'll have heard by now that Anna Sparks' ban has been overturned on appeal,' Jackson pressed. 'Any comment?'

Casey opened her mouth to start ranting but decided against it. Better to be gracious. 'None.' She clicked off the phone before he could ask any more awkward questions about Mrs Smith.

Kyle was smiling.

'Reporters. They're the same the world over. Have a drink, Casey. Enjoy yourself. You deserve it. You wiped the floor with Anna Sparks. You're a much better rider than she could ever be. Burghley, here we come.'

'Thanks, Kyle.' Casey raised her glass and smiled back. 'I could get used to this – the high life.'

Kyle let out a groan. 'Trust her to rain on our parade.'

The partying folk spilling out of the lorry had all stopped in mid-sentence, drink or gesture. They were riveted by a lonely figure walking dispiritedly across the busy lorry park. She was wearing a white polo-shirt with a grass strain on the back and leading a skewbald gelding.

Casey was puzzled. 'Who is she? Why is everyone staring?'

Kyle was incredulous. 'You don't recognise her? That's Anna Sparks, your old rival.'

Casey gave a snort of laughter. 'You're joking?'

'She got what was coming to her. She treated everyone like dirt on the way up and now she's having to eat it on the way down.'

As the girl drew nearer, Casey saw that it was indeed Anna Sparks. She'd piled on weight. Her heart-shaped face was puffy. She was still pretty and smartly dressed but she was not the ravishing beauty she had been when she ruled the circuit as one of the finest young riders in the world.

Her skewbald was fit and lean and had a quality look about him, but he hardly compared to her previous horse, Rough Diamond. He was caked in mud and rather poorly turned out. Despite this, his head was up and he looked quite pleased with himself.

'Seems as if a large part of Ms Sparks' success was her daddy's millions,' said Marsha, appearing at Casey's side with a beer. 'Now that they're not speaking and she doesn't have the best horses money can buy and an entourage to take care of them, she's discovering that eventing isn't quite so easy. Today she started last and finished last.'

Anna's pale gold hair, once a cascading mane, had been cut shoulder-length. Her fringe fell messily across her face. As she passed the lorry, she lifted a hand in a small wave. Nobody waved back, although a few people giggled and one of the riders shouted: 'It's the great Anna Sparks! Quick, somebody call the RSPCA.'

'Don't worry, it looks as if she's off the diet pills,'

Marsha said in a loud voice. 'That means there'll be no outbreaks of violence. Not today, at any rate.'

Everyone laughed, including Kyle. Casey was about to join in when Anna glanced up and their eyes met. Anna was the first to drop her gaze. She hurried away, pulling her painted horse behind her.

'The funniest part,' said Casey when she talked to Peter on the phone later, 'was when she went over to this funny little horsebox. It was so unglamorous and out of character. We all laughed till we cried. Do you remember when she used to have that huge luxury lorry that was the same make as Andrew Nicholson's? How the mighty have fallen.'

There was silence on the other end of the line.

'Are you still there?' asked Casey. 'Peter? Hello?'

'I'm here.'

'What do you think? Isn't it hilarious?'

'Do I think it's hilarious that a girl who is plainly suffering is turned into a laughing stock? No, frankly, I don't. Can you not see that what you did to Anna Sparks this evening was an exact replay of what she did to you at Brigstock two and a half years ago when she made fun of you and Storm and the donkey van you travelled in?'

'No,' Casey said coldly. 'I can't. That's different.'

'In what way is it different?'

'It just is. Whose side are you on, anyway? You haven't even congratulated me. We won, Peter. You're supposed to be happy.'

13

BARBARA MACCLESFIELD, HEAD nurse at the Primrose Valley Hospice, followed Mrs Smith into room 312 and watched as her newest resident deposited her meagre luggage on top of the chest of drawers. If you could call it luggage. Not counting an ethnic rucksack that doubled as her handbag, Angelica Smith's worldly possessions consisted of one large carpetbag, Kashmiri in origin, which had faded over time. She looked as if she'd recently disembarked from a ship originating in the Far East. Her clothes were equally exotic. In spite of the summer heat, she was wearing, over her Indian cotton dress, a coat that made her look as if she was auditioning for a role in *Joseph and the Amazing Technicolor Dreamcoat*.

'It's from Tibet,' explained Mrs Smith. 'I went there with my father as a teenager. Divine place.'

Beneath the window was a bed covered with a white sheet, pink blanket and pink candlewick cover, all made with military neatness. The remainder of the cramped room was taken up by a chest of drawers, a cupboard, a chair and a pale blue rug to match the walls. A television with an extending arm was bolted to the wall.

The only personal touch was a freshly picked daisy sitting in a glass on the chest of drawers. A pair of disposable white slippers, still in cellophane, sat on the mat beside the bed.

'You're an economical packer, I must say,' remarked Nurse Macclesfield. 'Most people bring everything but the kitchen sink when they come here – grandfather clocks, cats and enough books to fill the British Library.'

Mrs Smith smiled. 'This is it. Didn't think I'd need anything else.'

The nurse gestured towards a painting of a ship battling a gale in a tumultuous green ocean. Just looking at it made Mrs Smith feel seasick. 'Knocking nails into the wall is not permitted, but if you'd like to take down that picture and replace it with one of your own, feel free.'

Mrs Smith opened her carpetbag and lifted out a photograph of Casey. When choosing which to bring, she could have selected any number of shots of Casey soaring over fences, doing dressage, or kissing the Badminton trophy. But the one she loved most was a black and white one taken about a year after Mrs Smith had started working with her. Storm was still on the thin side and lacking in muscle tone, and Casey's collar was sticking up and her hair awry but, to Mrs Smith, they were beautiful in their innocence.

The photograph had been taken by Peter in the days when he and Casey were only friends, but the feelings he had for her were evident in the framing of the image. He'd captured horse and girl leaning together, forehead to forehead. Unaware that she was being photographed, Casey had her arms around Storm's neck and her eyes closed.

It was a picture of love, taken with love.

Whenever Mrs Smith glanced at it she was struck by how impossibly young Casey looked. Placing it on the bedside table, she wondered for the thousandth time whether it had been a mistake to agree to teach a naive young girl how to compete with the best in such a high-risk sport. Perhaps it had all been too much, too soon.

'What a wonderful photo,' cried Nurse Macclesfield. 'Is that your granddaughter?'

'No, that's Casey. She's my best friend. The horse's name is Storm Warning. He and Casey were the youngest ever Badminton champions.'

'I do enjoy a game of badminton,' said the nurse, misunderstanding. She'd never heard of eventing and would not have known a Derby winner from a Clydesdale. 'I'm not much good at ball sports on the whole, but I find that shuttlecocks are more visible and travel slower. Not at the Olympics, of course, but generally.'

She tailed off. 'You must have led a terribly exciting life.'

Mrs Smith looked away. 'Casey and Storm were my life.'

'Will she be coming to see you – your friend?'

'She doesn't know I'm here. I didn't want to worry her. She's busy, you see. She has Burghley coming up and the pressure is immense.'

Nurse Macclesfield pursed her lips. 'I understand. They're all busy nowadays, the young ones. However, I'm sure she'd want to know that this is where you'll be, you know, from now on. I can set you up on email and you can get in touch.'

'No!' said Mrs Smith with a finality that brooked no discussion.

Not wanting to upset a resident on her first day, Nurse Macclesfield said anxiously: 'I do hope you like it here. We'll do our best to take care of you.'

Suddenly weary, Mrs Smith sank down on the chair. It seemed a shame to disturb the crease-free bed. 'Are all of the patients at Primrose—?'

'We prefer to call you residents,' interjected the nurse.

'Residents – is this really where they come to die? Do people simply sit around waiting for the curtain to descend on their lives?'

'I wouldn't put it in quite that way. We'll do our best to help you to continue to enjoy life for as long as you can. How long that is, varies so much from individual to individual. Every now and then, we see a miracle and it's lovely when it happens, but it's best to be prepared. For some people, sadly, there really is no hope.'

'There's always hope – if not in body, then in spirit,' Mrs Smith said with feeling.

Nurse Macclesfield perked up. 'Of course there is. That's our philosophy too. For that reason, we have a full programme of activities. There is ballroom dancing, bridge, Pilates, chess and the perennially popular knitting club. I know it might not feel that way right now, but you still have a lot to live for.'

As the door shut behind her, Mrs Smith shuddered.

Somehow she survived a glutinous dinner and a screening of *It's a Wonderful Life*, followed, next morning, by a breakfast of watery scrambled eggs and tinned mushrooms. But by 10.38 a.m., she was climbing the walls. So far she'd turned down an early morning Pilates class, two card games and an invitation to knit a Highland terrier.

For people who are supposed to be on their last legs, these Primrose Valley residents have way too much energy, Mrs Smith thought uncharitably.

Temporarily freed from the pain that had crippled her, she found her restless mind returning constantly to

Storm and Casey. Casey, she knew, had already moved on. Mrs Smith detested technology and could barely operate a mobile phone, but the guilt she felt at abandoning Casey and jeopardising her career had driven her to an internet café. With assistance, she'd managed to access *New Equestrian* magazine's online site. What she read had devastated her.

When Mrs Smith looked up Casey's results, she'd hoped to find that her former pupil was doing reasonably well. Discovering that Casey had cruised to victory on Roxy barely a month after Mrs Smith left her was a blow. But the killing part had been Casey's words. It was bad enough that she attributed her success to the arrogant Kyle West and described him as a 'magician'. But then she added insult to injury by saying it was the 'best thing I have ever done'.

The agony Mrs Smith experienced as she digested the implication that she'd been a negative force in Casey's life was worse than anything the cancer had thrown at her.

And it was cancer. That much had been confirmed by the oncologist, Andrew Mutandwa, when she'd walked into his office the day after walking out on Casey.

'*Why?*' he kept asking her, near apoplectic with distress over her new test results. 'Why did you do it, Angelica?'

She shrugged. 'I had no choice.'

'Everybody has a choice. What I fail to understand is why yours was not your own health but mad, neck-breaking horse competitions. If you'd allowed us to start chemotherapy or radiotherapy five months ago, we would be looking at a very different outcome. I'm not saying that we'd have been able to save you. But with the right treatment we could have extended your life by years. Now you have months.'

'How many months?' Mrs Smith asked calmly. He wasn't telling her anything that she didn't expect to hear.

Mr Mutandwa looked more ill than she did. Originally from Zambia, he found these types of conversations almost more distressing than his patients did. Before answering, he retreated behind his desk and drew comfort from the wood-framed photo of his wife and children.

'I can't sugarcoat this for you, Angelica. You don't have much time. It is not an exact science and I don't like to put a number on it, but if I were you I would start saying goodbye to my loved ones.'

Mrs Smith emerged from the hospital feeling curiously relieved. For months she'd been unable to give a name to the monster destroying her from within. Now she could. Not only that but she had a shopping bag full of pills designed to eliminate the worst of the pain. All her life, Mrs Smith had spurned conventional medicine in favour of alternative treatments. Overnight that had changed. Now as she swallowed the tablets that stopped the spasms that sometimes ripped through her body with hurricane force, she felt that no amount of gold could compensate the sainted humans who made painkillers.

'By refusing to acknowledge my letters and face up to the truth about your disease sooner, you've effectively launched a grenade in your abdomen,' the specialist had bluntly informed her. 'Now you're going to have to endure the consequences.'

Mrs Smith had decided that she didn't like Mr Mutandwa after all. A little sugarcoating never hurt anyone.

Sitting on the fluffy bedcover at Primrose Valley, she paged through her red notebook. She had five such notebooks. They contained every detail of Casey's training schedule going back to the first morning at Hope Lane Riding Centre, when Storm was still a bag of bones and Casey a gawky fifteen-year-old in stretched breeches.

Mrs Smith opened the red notebook to a fresh page. During the night she'd had a flash of inspiration. For some time now she'd been very much on the side of those who believed that the removal of the steeplechase and roads and tracks sections at CCI****four-star events had unintended consequences for the horses' performance. The long format was too long but the short format was too short. Unable to sleep, Mrs Smith had come up with a way to redress the balance. Feeling more alive than she had in weeks, she urgently jotted down key points.

Mid-sentence, her pen paused.

'What are you doing, Angelica?' she asked herself. 'Casey no longer has any use for you or your eccentric ideas. You're a sad old fool. Read a book or take up knitting. Forget eventing. It's history.'

In the corridor outside her room, there was a squeak of wheels. Mrs Smith had been at the hospice less than twenty-four hours but already she was familiar with the sound of her neighbour's oxygen trolley. There was a timid knock at the door.

Mrs Smith set aside the notebook. If her room hadn't been on the second floor, she would have hopped out of the window and made a run for it.

'How about joining us for a 3 p.m. game of Monopoly?' rasped Irma Irving, trailing more tubes than an octopus.

Mrs Smith hesitated but it wasn't as if she had anything better to do. Board games were her new Badminton. 'Love to,' she said. 'Thanks for asking.'

14

O N A HOT summer's night in Gloucestershire, Casey sat on a garden bench watching fireworks scream into the starry sky and explode in a dazzle of scarlet. The man paying for both the party and the light show was Casper Leyton, multimillionaire owner of one of the biggest eventing studs in the United Kingdom. His daughter was a protégé of Kyle's and it was through Kyle that Casey had received an invitation. She'd jumped at the chance to go. Leyton's parties were legendary.

'You lucky thing,' cried Marsha, Sam Tide's groom, when Casey told her. 'Last year I spent so much time begging Sam to take me that in the end he agreed to pretend I was his date. I saw three Hollywood stars, half a dozen top riders letting their hair down, that delicious boy who won *The X Factor*, two Olympic rowers and a Russian gymnast. I could have died of happiness.'

The smoke from the fireworks mingled with smoke from the barbecue and swirled around the beautiful people dancing and chatting on the terrace. Stone steps led down to a heated swimming pool. Already that evening a couple of bikini-clad starlets had leapt into the water. The barbecue had been set up on a raised deck at the rear of the pool. There were platters of lobsters and langoustines, a hog on a spit and every kind of salad, vegetable dish and dessert imaginable. An ice sculpture of a unicorn, melting in the heat, regarded the scene imperiously.

Before Casey had won Badminton, she'd always wondered what it would be like to be part of the elite echelon of riders who were invited to the best parties and events. Their lives seemed impossibly glamorous. Now she was among them. Not that many of them knew who she was. A couple of people had congratulated her on her success and a drunk had offered her an obscene amount of money to part with Storm, but most guests looked past her or through her. The women were universally thin, tanned and coiffed. The men radiated power and assurance. Their Rolex watches winked in the lights. One lady, assuming Casey was a waitress, had asked her to fetch a drink.

Kyle had barely spoken to her since they arrived. Each time she spotted him, he was with a different girl and they were all stunning. 'Don't get any ideas about fancying Kyle,' Hannah had warned her. 'You'll only get hurt. Girls are all over him all the time and he's very polite and charming to them, but they make the mistake of thinking he's interested in them. Take it from me, they're dead wrong.'

Casey had laughed off this speech, putting it down to Hannah's fairly obvious crush on Kyle, but now she wasn't so sure. From this angle, it looked a lot like flirting.

She did her best to convince herself that it didn't bother her. Their relationship was purely business. Strictly speaking, they weren't even friends. She didn't want to think about the chemistry that had swirled around his sports car as he drove her to the party earlier, or the feeling she'd got when he put the top down and the wind blew through his hair.

All in all it had been a week that would have once been beyond her wildest fantasies. Thanks to Equi-Flow, she'd been invited to spend a day watching the Duke of Essex Polo Grand Prix in Hylands Park and enjoying a gourmet picnic. Ed Lashley-Jones had been cock-a-hoop about her weekend victory and had introduced her to lots of stylish aristocrats and celebrities, not one of whom she recognised. They didn't recognise her either, but such was Ed's enthusiasm that they dutifully fawned over her and bared sparkling white teeth.

The problem had come when Casey refused to agree to give a course of riding lessons to Candi's whiney teenage son.

'I'm sorry,' she said. 'I would if I could, but I'm in the midst of preparing for the Burghley Horse Trials and I'm working flat out. It's crucial that I focus.'

'But you have time to attend parties,' Lashley-Jones said pointedly. 'Might I remind you, Casey, that sponsorship is not all take, take, take. You have to give back some time, otherwise our shareholders will start to ask questions about why we're investing in you.'

He'd apologised later, but Casey was unnerved. Mrs Smith had been right. Ed and his cronies were parasites.

Watching a rocket curve into the night sky and burst into pink stars, she wondered what Peter was doing. Was he missing her as much as she missed him? Or was the Irish girl on his course, the one he'd described as 'so pretty that nobody could believe it when Orla also turned out to be a wickedly good farrier,' keeping him company?

But no, Peter wasn't like that. She'd trust him with her life. He loved her. With Peter she'd never once felt inadequate, the way she did now. Quite the reverse. He always, always made her feel good about herself.

Well, mostly. She hadn't felt good since he'd had a go at her over Anna Sparks. Quite why he'd stuck up for Anna, Casey couldn't fathom. Ms Sparks had treated him appallingly in the days when he used to shoe Rough Diamond and her other horses. But then that was one of the things Casey loved about Peter. He always looked for the best in people.

That said, he would not have enjoyed this party. It

wasn't his scene at all. Peter was the grandson of a Welsh sheep farmer and he was resolutely down to earth. If he'd been here now, he'd be wanting to leave. 'What's happening to you, Casey?' she could hear him saying. 'These are the kind of people you used to despise.'

'Enjoying yourself?'

Kyle loomed out of the darkness and flopped down beside her. He was wearing an open-necked white shirt, black trousers and Italian shoes. By some distance, he was the most gorgeous guy at the party. Casey inched away surreptitiously. The closer he came to her, the faster her heart skipped.

'I'm having a fabulous time,' said Casey in a bid to convince herself that she was doing just that. 'How about you? You seem to be flavour of the month.'

Kyle leaned forward, his tanned forearms resting on his thighs. His gaze was on the increasing revelry at the swimming pool.

'Is that what I am – flavour of the month? What happens when it's someone else's turn?' He said it lightly but there was a bitter note in his tone.

'Sorry. It was a flippant thing to say and not what I meant at all.'

'No, it's true. One slip-up and all this could be snatched away.'

He straightened and put an arm along the back of the bench. Casey's skin tingled as his hand brushed her shoulder. His face looked boyish and vulnerable in the moonlight. 'Ever get imposter syndrome, Casey?'

'If you're asking do I ever worry that someone is going to tap me on the shoulder one day and tell me that there's been a giant mistake – girls like me don't become eventing stars – then the answer is yes. All the time. I look at riders like Mary King and think I must be delusional to imagine I might ever be in their league. Competing at this level was my dream, but now that I'm here I worry that I don't deserve it.'

A firework popped and crackled, scrawling champagne-coloured graffiti across the night sky.

'Yes, you do,' Kyle assured her, 'and you have the results to prove it. I can relate to how you feel though. Sometimes I wake up in a cold sweat, convinced that my pupils will realise that there are other, better coaches and one by one they'll leave me.'

Casey laughed. 'I think we should both agree that we are where we're meant to be and enjoy it while it lasts. Anyway, you've convinced me that you're going to help me and Storm win the Grand Slam. They'll have to give you the Golden Horseshoe Award after that.'

He grinned and the arrogance returned to his body language as if he were donning a cloak. 'They will. Hey, don't pay any attention to me. I'm having a moment, that's all. Happens sometimes. Wanna get out of here?'

Two days later, Casey moved Storm to Rycliffe Manor for a week of intensive work. At White Oaks she'd been doing interval training with him and had been astounded at how rapidly her big silver horse shed pounds and regained his fitness.

Even Morag was impressed. 'I guess it's something to do with muscle memory. You've done so much work with him over the past year that I suppose six weeks off is nothing to a horse like him. His champion genes were simply lying dormant, waiting for a chance to burst forth.'

As much as she tried to talk herself out of it, Casey had reservations about taking Storm to Rycliffe Manor. It was a breathtakingly lovely estate and the facilities were second to none, but the incident with the dogs had tainted the place for her. Whenever she thought about the cross-country course, the dogs came bursting into her imagination and pounced on Storm, fangs bared.

But move to Rycliffe Manor she did, because Kyle was her teacher and he and the estate came as a package. She was also keen to get working with Storm because it would take her mind off Roxy. A week after the Westwood Classic, Jennifer Stewart had rung to say that she'd sold the mare and would be coming to pick her up the following morning. Casey had been gutted. She'd come to adore Roxy and had convinced herself that Jennifer would realise that she, Storm and Roxy belonged together. Parting them would be cruel.

Sadly, like many people who viewed horses as

investments rather than intelligent, feeling beings, Jennifer never let sentiment get in the way of a good deal.

'But we've bonded,' Casey told her, as she led Jennifer to Roxy's stable and demonstrated the transformation in the mare. 'Look how gentle and amazing she is. She's a pleasure to work with. When she arrived here, she was a biting, kicking menace. She tried to crush me against the wall when I attempted to saddle her. Now look at her.'

She gave Roxy a couple of Polos. 'She's only just settled in and found her feet. It seems such a shame to move her. Besides, she's besotted with my horse, Storm. They're like two lovebirds. Give me another couple of months and I'll try to find some more money and give you a better price for her.'

Jennifer, who'd come straight from the office and was wearing a power suit in grey and cream, ran an appraising hand over Roxy's shining bay coat. She gave her a slap on the rump that made the mare jump with fright.

'I hear what you're saying but I can't do it, Casey. I have a buyer in hand and that's worth two in the bush. But I do agree that she's improved beyond all recognition. That Kyle West is a wonder. I don't know how he's transformed her in such a short time. Please thank him when you see him.'

Irritated that Jennifer had immediately leapt to the conclusion that the change in Roxy was down to

Kyle's influence, Casey made a big show of cuddling Roxy and kissing her goodbye after loading her in the horsebox.

'She's always been an odd one, Lady Roxanne,' said Jennifer as they lifted the ramp and bolted it shut. 'That's what I told the journalist who called, doing an article on you. I said Roxy's character had been affected by what happened at the home of the people who bred her. They had these great big dogs. I'm not sure what breed they were, but something scary. Unbeknown to their owners, these mutts had dug a hole under the fence and would routinely go into the paddock where the yearlings were kept and terrorise Roxy.

'Apparently, the family had a teenage son who didn't like horses who found this funny. He used to sit on the fence and laugh. The parents went berserk when they found out. Roxy was sold twice before I bought her as an investment horse. At that stage, I was ignorant of her background and had great hopes for her, but her problems soon became too much for me. I have a demanding job and didn't have time to deal with her. I was in a quandary as to what to do when I read that you were looking for a ride while Storm Warning was resting. I'm glad it worked out so well.'

Absorbed in her story, she didn't notice that Casey had stopped listening. Vicious dogs had terrorised Roxy as a yearling and it was vicious dogs that had triggered the chain of events that had led to her transformation. If it was a coincidence, it was a striking one.

'Who was the journalist?' Casey asked casually. 'Which publication were they from?'

Jennifer Stewart jingled her car keys. 'Do you know, I'm not sure. *Horse and Hound*, I think, but I may be mistaken. It was weeks ago now.'

It was a warm day but Casey was suddenly freezing. She tried to remember the timeline – what had happened when. 'Before I won the Westwood Classic?'

'Oh, well before. I don't recall the woman's name either. She did tell me but I've forgotten.'

She drove away with Roxy neighing desperately, bewildered that she was being wrenched from Casey and Storm, her new best friends. Casey didn't stop crying for an hour.

Lonely in the guest room at Rycliffe Manor that night, she tried calling Peter. She needed to reconnect to him. He might have been only a few hundred miles away in Ireland, but it felt as if he was on the moon.

Peter would tell her that she was letting her imagination run away with her. He didn't like Kyle, but he was man enough to put that aside and reassure her that she was doing the right thing bringing Storm to Rycliffe Manor. That, of course, people didn't go around engineering dog attacks as a training method. That nobody would do that unless they were psychotic.

The phone was answered on the second ring not by her boyfriend but by a girl with a huskily sexy voice and an Irish accent.

Casey was thrown. 'Umm, I think I might have dialled the wrong number. I'm trying to reach Peter Rhys.'

The girl said breathily: 'This is Peter's phone. He forgot to take it with him when he went out. Who may I say called?'

'My name's Casey.' Then she added for good measure, 'His girlfriend.'

There was a giggle. 'His *girlfriend*? Oh, how sweet. He hasn't mentioned you. I'm Orla, by the way. We're doing Alejandro Hall's course together.'

Casey digested the information that, after a month in Ireland, Peter hadn't told the prettiest girl on his course that he was in a relationship.

'Peter will be back soon,' the husky voice was saying. 'He's only nipped out to get us a pizza.'

Us?

'Everyone else went off to the pub, but he and I felt like a quiet night in. I'll tell him that you rang.'

Casey switched off her phone and for a brief, angry moment wondered why it was that she was trying so hard to resist Kyle when her boyfriend was getting cosy with Orla.

15

*H*ELP ME, CASEY! *Help me!*
Casey sat bolt upright in her bed at Rycliffe Manor Equestrian Centre. She'd forgotten to shut the window and the room was like the Arctic but she was bathed in sweat. It wasn't a dream, she was sure of it. She'd heard Mrs Smith call out to her as clearly as if she'd been standing before her.

With shaking hands she dialled Mrs Smith's number. Mrs Smith rarely, if ever, answered her phone, and would never dream of doing so at 2.45 a.m., but if she was as desperate as she sounded perhaps she would. Her hopes were dashed when it went straight to voicemail.

Casey debated whether to call her dad, who was back from Italy, but decided against it. If she rang him in the dead of night and said she was hearing voices, he'd think she'd lost her mind. Better to at least wait until he'd had breakfast.

She lay back down and did her best to convince herself that the voice had been a product of her own guilty conscience. She was haunted by the way it had ended with Mrs Smith, haunted by not knowing what had become of her. Mrs Smith had never done anything that was expected of her and could at this moment be at a yoga retreat on a mountaintop in Kerala, but again and again Casey returned to the worst-case scenario – Mrs Smith desperately ill and alone.

Her alarm rang, blasting the thought from her tired mind. In an effort to increase her riding experience, Kyle had entered her in the Aston-le-Walls Horse Trials in Northamptonshire. She'd be riding a big black bruiser of a horse called Assassin's Code. Casey had set her alarm for 3 a.m., even though she wasn't actually required to do anything. Rycliffe Manor's star clients were not required to do any pre-event grooming. All plaiting and preparation would be done for her by a groom and Assassin would be boxed and ready to leave at 5 a.m. sharp.

Casey had at first been so taken by the novelty of not having to get up at the usual unearthly hour that she'd agreed – albeit with a twinge of conscience. Mrs Smith was a firm believer that the pre-show routine was an essential part of the rider-horse bonding experience. Now she was glad she'd changed her mind. It meant that she could do an hour's lateral work with Storm and ensure that he was settled and happy before she left him for the day. It would also take her mind off the question of Mrs Smith until she could ring her dad. She planned to ask him if the Hackney grapevine had any news of Mrs Smith's whereabouts.

'Well, this is very upsetting,' said Roland Blue, who was making scrambled eggs when she rang him from a motorway service station en route to Northamptonshire. 'It's bad enough that the two of you have parted company and you know my feelings on *that* subject. But I didn't know you weren't in contact.'

'Don't give me a hard time, Dad. I feel awful enough as it is. Can you please just do me a favour and try to find out where she is? I'm worried about her.'

Pans clanged in the background. 'I'll see what I can find out, Pumpkin, but it's concerning that she's simply vanished. As a matter of fact, I was going to text you to ask for her new contact details. The other day I passed her old flat and there was a For Sale sign out the front. What happened between the two of you, anyway? I thought you were the best of friends.'

There was a knot of fear in Casey's gut. Where was Mrs Smith? Somehow Casey had convinced herself that she was back living in her Victorian apartment in London's East End, feeding strays and drinking chai at the Tea Garden the way she had when Casey met her. 'We were friends. We *are*. Dad, I have to go. We're on our way to Aston-le-Walls and everyone's waiting for me.'

'Sorry,' she said to Kyle as she clambered into the lorry. 'I needed to speak to my dad about something.'

When Kyle had first suggested that he travel to and from the event with her, Casey had been thrilled at the thought of having company in the big lorry. But so far that morning he'd hardly said a word. He'd been sweet to her when he did speak but for the most part he seemed moody and distracted.

Now he frowned. 'Your dad? Do you get on with him?'

Casey was surprised that he was surprised. 'I adore my dad. He's all the family I have in the world. Well, apart from Mrs Smith, but she—' She broke off. She didn't want to go there.

Kyle didn't appear to notice. 'Can I ask you a personal question?'

'Depends.'

'You don't have to answer if you don't want to. Your father – he's a convicted burglar, right?'

Casey tensed. 'Yes, he is. But he did his time and now he's a successful tailor.'

'Do you mind if I ask what he did?'

Casey took a deep breath. She rarely talked about it and it never got any easier when she did.

'About five years ago, he fell in with a dodgy crowd. They convinced him to join them on a job to rob a multimillionaire. We were battling to make ends meet and it wasn't hard for them to persuade Dad that this man would hardly miss a few thousand. But on the night of the robbery, everything went horribly wrong. The owner of the house woke up and ended up attacking Dad with a poker. The police came just as Dad knocked the man out with a lamp in an attempt to defend himself. His so-called mates escaped scot free. Dad got eight months. Volunteering at a local riding school and my friendship with Mrs Smith were about the only things that got me through it.'

Kyle was watching her intently. 'And you forgave him?'

Casey wondered where this was going. 'He's human. People make mistakes and he paid for his. I was angry with him for a long time, especially when the tabloids got wind of what he'd done and it was all over the papers. But eventually I forgave him. He's tried so hard to rebuild his life and make it up to me. Added to which, he helped me rescue Storm from the knacker's yard. I'll always love him for that.'

Kyle opened his window and let a blast of cold motorway air into the lorry's cab. 'You're amazing, Casey Blue. I could never be like you. If I found out that my father had committed a crime, I could never forgive him. It's not that I'd cut him off or anything. I'd stay in touch with him or even stay with him. But the horror of what he'd done, the ruined lives, would stay with me till my dying day.'

It was not the most cheerful conversation Casey had ever had and she was relieved when Kyle excused himself not long after they arrived at Washbrook Farm and went off to see another client. She was making herself the first of many cappuccinos and reading the names on the start sheet when she heard a muffled sob.

Outside, she saw nobody in distress. It was a blustery blue day, perfect for riding, and the lorry park was already packed with immaculately turned out horses and riders and grooms in various states of anxiety or excitement. Casey was about to return to her cappuccino when she heard the sound again.

The lorry beside hers was temporarily deserted. Walking round to the other side, she was startled to see Anna Sparks in tears. The reason was obvious. Her skewbald's plaits were sticking out in all directions. He looked like a pony punk rocker.

When Anna glanced up to find Casey watching her, she was mortified. Recovering, she wiped her eyes roughly and glared. 'Enjoying yourself? Bet you are. What could be more entertaining than watching Anna Sparks finally getting her comeuppance? She's so used to having an entourage that she can't even plait a mane. Well, Casey Blue, it's your lucky day. You're about to see something even more amusing. Very shortly I'll be disqualified as a no-show because I have no hope of being ready for the dressage. The person who'd promised to help me hasn't shown up. Happy now?'

'Don't be ridiculous,' said Casey, striding over and

162

taking the elastics and thread from Anna's unresisting hands. 'If I wanted to make you suffer all I'd have to do is ride better than you. Now shove over and let me redo your plaits. You're going about it all wrong. Watch and learn. Mrs Smith taught me and she's a genius at it. She's also a perfectionist. When I first attempted to plait Storm's mane, she made me redo it about eighty times. In the end my hands were so sore I could barely hold the reins.'

She undid the botched plaits, combed out the horse's mane and started again. 'What's his name?' she asked more kindly.

'Chocolate.'

'You're kidding?' Casey caught herself mid-giggle and told herself off. Anna was an evil wicked girl who'd injured Storm and gone out of her way to mock and deride Casey. She was not to be trusted.

'If I'm going to do this for you, I've got to concentrate,' she said huffily. 'Why don't you go and do some stretches or something? Mrs Smith always says that it's as important for the rider to be warmed up as it is for the horse.'

If, an hour earlier, someone had told her that she'd be plaiting the mane of her sworn enemy's horse and offering her advice, Casey would have fallen on the floor laughing. She'd have said that she'd rather walk barefoot on hot coals. But faced with Anna's distress she found herself incapable of hating her. Odder still, she felt a perverse pride when Anna posted a good dressage result, despite having only had five minutes to warm up.

Kyle was not pleased that Casey almost made herself late for the dressage in the process.

'Where were you?' he demanded. 'I came looking for you and you'd disappeared. I'll be very annoyed if Assassin performs poorly in the dressage. It's his best discipline. What were you doing?'

'I'm sorry,' said Casey, reluctant to admit to helping Anna. 'I got talking to someone and lost track of time.'

Fortunately, she performed well in the dressage, finishing a couple of places ahead of her old rival. The show jumping was less of a success. Assassin had a habit of accelerating after every jump. He'd fling up his head and almost bash Casey in the nose, making it difficult for her to keep him on line. Impossible to slow, he completely misjudged the wall and ended up crashing through it.

'There were one or two good bits but on the whole it was a mess,' Kyle said when Casey exited the arena. 'Don't blame Assassin. It was your fault. With horses like him, the key is to work on problem areas in the collecting ring. When you ride circles, be disciplined about them. Don't drift. Ask him to lower his head and gradually you'll find that he takes the contact down, freeing up his back. Because he feels more secure, you'll find his canter much easier to ride.'

Casey was so relieved that Kyle was no longer upset with her for being late to warm-up for the dressage that she didn't like to point out it would have been helpful if he'd told her that when she still had time to do something about it, and not after the event when she didn't.

She found Kyle's teaching good but inconsistent. It puzzled her that he could be lucid and insightful one minute and stubbornly blind the next. Take what happened in her lunch break, for instance. Casey was making them both cappuccinos in the back of the lorry and plotting how to improve her performance in the cross-country. She might have helped Anna Sparks – currently six places above her after only four faults in the show jumping – but she was fiercely determined to finish ahead of her.

'How would you feel about changing Assassin's bit?' Casey asked Kyle, who was sprawled on the lorry sofa in black breeches, Ariat boots and a white polo-shirt, looking impossibly attractive. His blond hair flopped over his face as he pored over *Eventing* magazine.

He didn't look up. 'Case, let's talk about this when we get home. I don't think it's a good plan to start changing things mid-event.'

'But what's your opinion? I have a feeling that his bit is making him unhappy and that's why he's pulling. He's desperate to escape it.'

Kyle tossed aside the magazine and took the mug of cappuccino from her. When she sat down beside him, he pushed his fringe from his blue eyes and gave her one of those looks that made her feel as if she'd developed a heart murmur. 'Did I ever tell you I think you're beautiful?'

'No, but I—'

'I know, I know. You have a boyfriend. Where is he? That's what I'm curious about. If you were mine, I'd never let you out of my sight.'

Casey jumped up and pretended to be looking for the sugar. She didn't want him asking probing questions about Peter, who still hadn't called her back. He knew she was competing at Aston-le-Walls and yet she'd not had so much as a text from him since leaving a message with the ravishing Orla. That was how Casey pictured the Irish girl: ravishing. She'd have silky dark tresses, a permanent tan and a stunning figure. Together with the seductive voice and Irish accent, she'd be hard to resist – especially on a quiet night in with a pizza.

'Peter's on a farrier's course in Ireland. With Alejandro Hall. He has to be away. He doesn't have a choice.'

'Everybody has a choice,' said Kyle. 'But don't worry. I'm not hitting on you. Well, maybe a little. Really, I just wanted you to know that I think you're very pretty. You're kind too, which is a lot more important.'

He glanced at his watch. 'Gosh, is that the time? I'm supposed to be meeting someone for a bite to eat. See you before the cross-country, Casey.'

It was only after he'd gone, leaving his untouched coffee cooling on the table, that Casey realised he'd evaded the conversation about the bit.

Without a change in tack the cross-country was, if anything, a more hair-raising experience than the show jumping. Assassin's owner was a farmer who had bigger biceps or more authority than Casey did. Either way, she was unable to do much more than steer as he flew around the course as if he was pursuing the leaders at the Grand National. By the end Casey was so drained that she was like a ragdoll in the saddle.

She had hoped that Kyle might be there at the finish, but he was nowhere in sight. 'Probably watching it on the monitors with some of the officials,' Assassin's groom consoled her. 'Easier to watch several riders at once.'

Casey had planned to help cool Assassin down, but the groom waved her away. 'Get yourself a cold drink. You look as if you need it.'

Casey found a stand selling milkshakes and sipped a strawberry one as she studied the scoreboard. There were still five or six riders to go, but barring a disaster she'd finish twenty-ninth. Anna Sparks was two places behind.

She was crossing the lorry park in search of Kyle when Anna came running up. 'Casey, wait. I don't know how to thank you. After the way I treated you, I wouldn't blame you if you hated me.'

Casey stopped. 'Let's get one thing straight. I did what I did for your horse, not for you. I wouldn't help you if you were the last girl in England.'

Anna's face fell. 'That's okay. I totally understand. If I were you, I'd feel the same way.'

'Great,' said Casey. 'At least we've cleared that up.' Then, as Anna continued to stand there, 'Look, no offence, but some things are hard to forget. See you around.'

Anna followed her. 'Casey, please. Let me say one thing. I'm sorry about Storm. You don't know how much. My father bought him without telling me, but that's no excuse. I knew that it would kill you to part with him and I went along with it anyway. I rode him and it was my fault that he was injured.'

Casey couldn't believe what she was hearing. For so long, she'd raged at Anna in her head. Never did she imagine that her arch-enemy would one day apologise to her in person or appear to show genuine remorse.

'I want to try to make it up to you and the only way I can think of is to warn you.'

'Warn me about what?'

'Whatever you do, don't let Storm go to Rycliffe Manor. Nothing is what it seems there, not even Kyle.'

Cold fury surged through Casey. She had to restrain herself from physically shaking the girl. 'Do you know that just for a moment you had me fooled? Idiot that I am, I was starting to believe that you'd changed. I guess I was wrong. You're the same stuck-up jealous liar you always were. Once a bitch, always a bitch.'

Anna went white. 'Casey, I'm not saying this to hurt you. I saw what they did to Mouse. He was never the same after he went there.'

Casey had a flash of déjà-vu. She was standing on

the stairwell at Rycliffe Manor listening to Kyle say accusingly to Ray: 'The way it worked with Mouse, you mean?' And Ray had responded: 'That wasn't my fault. The girl was out of control.'

'Casey, I'm not saying this out of jealousy. You have to believe me.'

Before Casey could think of a suitable retort, her phone buzzed in the pocket of her breeches. She snatched it out, hoping it was Peter. To her delight, Mrs Smith's number came up.

'You have no idea how happy I am to hear from you,' she cried joyfully.

But the voice on the line was not Mrs Smith's. 'Am I speaking to Casey Blue?'

A chill rippled through Casey. 'Yes, you are. Who is this?'

'Casey, my name is Barbara Macclesfield. I'm head nurse at the Primrose Valley Hospice in North London. I apologise for disturbing you – I understand you're very busy – but I wasn't sure who else to call. Angelica Smith has no next of kin and she said ... well, she described you as her best friend.'

'She ... she did?'

'I'm afraid I have bad news. Mrs Smith is gravely ill. She collapsed last night and is not responding to treatment.'

'What treatment?'

'For cancer. You do know she has cancer?'

The lorry park blurred before Casey's eyes. Dimly,

she was aware of Anna rushing forward to put an arm around her.

She said faintly: 'I'm in Northamptonshire but I'll be on my way as soon as I can find someone to drive me to a train station. Is she in hospital?'

'Sadly, it's much too late for that. I'm sorry to be blunt, Casey, but if you're going to come, it needs to be now. Angelica is dying.'

The phone fell from Casey's hand. She collapsed on the ground, sobbing uncontrollably.

Suddenly Kyle was there, lifting her into his arms. 'Get away from her,' he yelled at Anna. 'Haven't you caused enough damage? Casey, sweetheart, what's wrong? Sorry I couldn't get here any quicker, but don't worry. I'm here for you now.'

16

THE FIGURE LYING motionless beneath a pink duvet at the Primrose Valley Hospice was paper-white and birdlike, unrecognisable as the charismatic teacher who'd taken a penniless teenager and a knacker's yard horse and made them champions. She was hooked up to a drip and heavily sedated. On the bedside table was a black and white photograph of Casey and Storm.

At the sight of it Casey almost burst into tears, but she knew she had to stay strong for Mrs Smith's sake. 'How long has she been here?'

Nurse Macclesfield was rarely surprised by anything, but the slender, athletic girl regarding her with serious, storm-grey eyes was unlike any other teenager she'd come across. She had been brought to the hospice by a startlingly beautiful boy wearing black breeches and fabulous boots. As thrilling as it was to have a character who looked as if he'd stepped straight from the pages of a Jane Austen novel cross her path, Nurse Macclesfield had been thankful when Casey had sent him on his way with barely a backward glance. Several of the residents had weak hearts.

'Ten days,' she told Casey. 'Angelica has been with us for around ten days. At first she made an effort to join the other residents in card games and Pilates, but she became increasingly restless. She seemed obsessed with visiting book shops and libraries. I worried that she might be overdoing it, but she didn't want advice. There was nothing I could do. Primrose Valley is not a prison. Residents can come and go as they please, unless they have dementia or Alzheimer's. But in the case of someone like Angelica, how they choose to spend their last days is up to them.'

Casey looked up sharply. 'You mean, their last years?'

'No, I don't. We care for the terminally ill in the final stages of life. In most cases, that means months or weeks.'

Casey stared at her, not understanding. 'Are you saying that when Mrs Smith came here, she already knew she was dying?'

Nurse Macclesfield felt for her. She'd seen it before. Friends and relatives who were so caught up in their own frenetic lives that they didn't see what was in front of them until it was too late. 'She did know she was dying, yes.'

Casey sank onto on a chair. 'I don't understand why she didn't call me.'

'She said that you were too busy, that you had a horse event to prepare for. The Burghley Horse Trials, is it?'

A wave of nausea enveloped Casey. She'd shouted at Mrs Smith and told her that she'd never signed a document making her manager. Like a spoilt, selfish child, she'd raged: 'I choose the lorry!' She'd thoughtlessly compared Mrs Smith's increasing frailty with Kyle's youthful vigour when all the while Mrs Smith must have had the strength of ten lions to keep teaching and keep giving when her body was being ravaged by a killer disease.

Casey went over to the bed and gazed down at the woman she loved like a mother. She took Mrs Smith's hand in hers. 'How much time has she got left?'

'It's hard to say. Her specialist, Andrew Mutandwa, told her she had months, but it could be weeks or even days. Between you and me, I think it would help if she had a reason to go on living.'

It was then that Casey saw, poking out of Mrs Smith's rucksack, a red notebook. She knew what it was immediately. Throughout their time together, Mrs Smith had never gone anywhere without a journal. She kept meticulous records of every nuance of Casey and Storm's training programme, as well as nutritional notes and other critical information. They'd often paged through these diaries together, recalling particular sessions or looking up cross-country-course diagrams or measurements, so Casey didn't feel she was violating Mrs Smith's privacy now.

Opening it, she fully expected the last entry to correspond with the date Mrs Smith had left White Oaks. But the red notebook was virtually full. Page after page was filled with detailed plans for Storm's training schedule right up until the Burghley Horse Trials in September. That was astounding enough, but it was Mrs Smith's radical new theories on preparing for CCI**** four-star events that blew Casey's mind.

She closed the journal with a snap. 'Nurse Macclesfield, how long would it take you to get Mrs Smith's things together? She's coming home with me.'

'I'm afraid that won't be possible. She's too ill to be moved. Casey, I know it's hard to accept but she's dying.'

'That's exactly why I want her with me. If she stays here, she'll die quietly and quickly, surrounded by strangers. If she comes with me, I'll give her a reason to live. Whatever happens, she'll be with me and Storm. We're the ones who love her most.'

Nurse Macclesfield opened her mouth to object, but in the face of Casey's steel-eyed determination she knew she wouldn't get far. Besides, if her brief acquaintance with Angelica Smith had shown her anything it was that she was a free spirit whose flame had burned brightest when she talked about being on the horse circuit with Casey and Storm. If she were to survive, they might be the miracle she needed.

'Give me ten minutes,' she told Casey. 'I'll speak to the doctor and organise some transport for you. Now would you like a cup of sweet coffee? You're rocking on your feet.'

17

THE RUSTING GATES had been given a lick of paint and a climbing rose was blooming on a trellis outside the office, but in all other ways Hope Lane Riding Centre – known to all but Mrs Ridgley as Hopeless Lane – was unchanged. The same motley crew of learners bumped around on the same leaden-footed horses. Casey stopped to give a Polo to Patchwork, the woolly piebald cob she'd long ago attempted to coax over piles of junk in a bid to pretend she was riding at Badminton. She had hoped that Patchwork might remember her fondly, but he merely crunched the mints and stared vacantly into space.

'Humbling, isn't it, the way they move on and forget all about you,' said Mrs Ridgeley with her usual lack of tact. Unnoticed, the stocky, yellow-haired owner of the riding school had come up behind Casey as she walked along the line of horses. 'Fame means nothing to them. Doesn't mean a lot around here either.'

Casey met Mrs Ridgeley's gaze without flinching. Few people could have done a better job of running a riding school in one of London's roughest inner-city neighbourhoods and for that the woman had her respect, but Mrs Ridgeley had thought that Casey was out of her mind to rescue Storm and she'd made their lives much more difficult than was necessary. At the same time, Casey would be for ever grateful to her. Without the loan of Mrs Ridgeley's storeroom, which became his stable, Storm would have had to be put down or returned to the knacker's yard to be slaughtered.

She summoned a smile. 'Believe it or not, I didn't come here to gloat. I came to see how you were all doing and to find out if you needed a hand. I'll be staying with my father for a week or two. If you wanted me to give some free lessons or even muck out, I'd be glad to do it.'

'Casey Blue!' cried Gillian, Hopeless Lane's best instructor and one of Casey's favourite people. 'You haven't forgotten us. We miss you. We especially miss the entertainment factor provided by you and Storm in the early days. Remember that time he cleared a stack of show jumps and the water trough as if he were a scrawny Pegasus?'

'We definitely do not miss those days,' Mrs Ridgeley said firmly. 'Gillian, Casey here seems to think that the

177

customers of Hope Lane might benefit from her free services. She has even offered to muck out. What do you think?'

Gillian whooped with delight. 'Are you serious? That's made my day. Casey, you're on. How soon can you start?'

For Casey, it was comforting but also deeply unsettling to return to her roots. She realised with a sense of shame that she had not spent a night in her old home at No. 414 Redwing Towers, a council block every bit as grim and grey as she remembered, since she and Mrs Smith had moved to White Oaks in the lovely Kent countryside in spring the previous year.

As she walked the streets of her childhood, including the cacophonous, sometimes deadly 'Murder Mile', everything she'd done and achieved fell away. She felt anonymous. None of the immigrants, artists or city workers who flowed like a human tide through Hackney knew or could have cared less about Badminton or the Kentucky Three-Day Event. It was liberating.

Her father was beside himself with happiness to have her home, but he fretted constantly about Mrs Smith, installed in Casey's bedroom. Surrounded by Casey's old horse posters, she spent most of each day sleeping. Casey took her bowls of homemade minestrone and tried talking to her, but all she did was lie staring at the ceiling. She either couldn't speak or didn't want to.

'Surely she should be in hospital?' worried Roland Blue. 'She's depressed and terminally ill. She needs professional help.'

'Give her time,' said Casey. 'We're all the help that she needs. Well, she needs to be with horses too, but first she needs to be well enough to move.'

On the fifth day, when Mrs Smith seemed worse than ever, Casey took a bus to Dalston. It was a while since she'd been to the house of Janet, Mrs Smith's healer friend who'd twice saved Storm, but she remembered the number.

'*Cancer?*'

Janet, a voluptuous woman in an embroidered white kaftan, jingled her bracelets in agitation. She was sad but not surprised to hear of Mrs Smith's diagnosis or what had followed.

'Never did like being told what to do, Angelica. Always liked to take things one step too far. But I can't criticise her because I'm the same way. Even so it seems tragic that in choosing to embrace life in all its glory she must now pay the highest price.'

Casey fought back tears. 'So help her. If anyone can save her, it's you.'

'Oh, no,' said Janet. 'No, no, no. Cancer is beyond my scope, I'm afraid. Casey, I know it's hard but you'd probably do best to take Angelica back to the Primrose Valley Hospice. They're the experts with this sort of thing.'

Casey jumped to her feet. 'You don't believe a single word you've just said,' she said furiously. 'You believe quite the opposite. You're reluctant to step in because you're afraid of it going wrong. You think I'm expecting you to cure her. I'm not. But I am asking you to put yourself in her position. Given a choice between a slow death in a stifling hospice room, where the most dramatic thing that happens in any day is a game of Scrabble, or going out on a high, which would you go for?'

She took the red notebook from her bag and handed it to the older woman. Janet flicked through it in silence. 'She's written all of this in the time since the two of you parted?'

'Yes, and it's pure genius. I want to use it. Her strategy: I want to use it to train for Burghley.'

Janet's eyes widened. 'Are you suggesting what I think you're suggesting?'

'Uh-huh.'

'Far be it from me to question your sanity, but ... Oh, all right, I will question it. Have you lost your mind?'

Casey grinned. 'Probably, but you have to admit that I'm right.'

'It's risky.'

'I know.'

'You need to understand up front that I can do nothing to cure her cancer or slow the spread of the disease. All I can offer is something – a potion – that might, for a time, make her feel a little better.'

'Worked for Storm,' said Casey. 'Made him a champion.

No reason at all why it shouldn't do wonders for Mrs Smith.'

She slept in a sleeping bag beside Mrs Smith's bed that night, as she had every night for the past week. Or at least she would have slept if she could. Mostly she stared into the darkness, worrying first about Mrs Smith, who had swallowed Janet's green potion without comment and immediately dropped into a coma-like sleep, and next about Storm, alone at Rycliffe Manor.

Nothing is what it seems there, not even Kyle.

What if Anna hadn't been speaking out of envy or bitterness? What if she'd genuinely wanted to keep Casey from making a terrible mistake?

Regardless of Anna's motivation, Casey couldn't bear being apart from her precious horse. Since the day of his rescue he'd only ever been taken care of by her, Mrs Smith and, occasionally, Jin, a Chinese friend of Casey's from Hopeless Lane. Now he was alone in a strange place being looked after by Assassin's competent but rather vacant groom. It didn't exactly fill Casey with confidence.

She'd phoned Kyle twice to check on Storm. Kyle insisted he was fine.

'Like me he's missing you, but otherwise he's doing well. We've turned him out in the field so he can stretch his legs, but if we're going to have any chance at winning the Burghley Horse Trials he needs to get back into training asap. Ray has offered to ride him or lunge him. He feels that Storm has grown a little spoilt and accustomed to getting his own way and might benefit from someone with a different approach to yours in your absence.'

Casey had only just managed to stop herself from screaming: 'Don't you dare let that freak touch my horse!'

Controlling herself with difficulty she said, 'Under no circumstances is anyone to ride, school or do anything other than groom and feed Storm. I'll be back in a few days and we'll get to work.'

'Great. Let me know if you need anything in the meantime. How's Angelica?'

'She's making a great recovery,' Casey lied. It irritated her when Kyle referred to Mrs Smith by her first name and in such a familiar way.

'That's good to hear. The sooner you're back in the saddle the better. Oh, by the way, Joyce in the office said that Peter called, looking for you. She didn't know he was your boyfriend so she told him that you were away for a couple of weeks and couldn't be contacted. But I expect that by now you've told him where you are.'

Casey had murmured something unintelligible into the phone and hung up as soon as she could. That was another thing she was worried about – Peter. She'd sent him two texts about Mrs Smith and left a message saying that she was at her father's flat and would love to talk to him. Agonisingly, she hadn't received a single response. But if he'd tried to ring her at Rycliffe Manor, surely that meant he still loved her?

Scrolling down to his number, she'd pressed call. His phone went straight to voicemail. The temperature in Casey's heart sank to zero.

Lying on the floor beside Mrs Smith, she struggled to get comfortable in the sleeping bag. Everything hurt. When sleep finally came, it was fractured by images of Orla clinging to Peter with her long red nails, and Ray lunging a terrified Storm.

And all the while Anna's warning was stuck on repeat in her head. 'Whatever you do, don't let Storm go to Rycliffe Manor ... I saw what they did to Mouse. He was never the same after he went there.'

Who was Mouse?

She was woken by a sliver of sunlight sliding under the blind. Even before she opened her eyes, she knew that something had changed. The energy in the room felt different.

She hauled herself upright. Mrs Smith was sitting in the armchair watching her. The colour had returned to her cheeks. She was desperately thin, but her eyes were bright.

183

'God, how I've missed you, Casey Blue.'

Casey burst out laughing. Jumping out of her sleeping bag, she flung her arms around Mrs Smith. 'Not half as much as I've missed you.'

She pulled back and said sternly: 'Don't ever do that to me again – vanish and not tell me where you are.'

'I won't, I promise.'

'I'm sorry,' Casey said. 'I'm sorry for being so selfish and self-absorbed that I didn't notice you were ill. How you kept it from me for so long, I can't imagine. You must have been in agony. And on top of everything you had me behaving like a brat. I lost the plot for a while. Fame went to my head.'

'Oh, I wouldn't go that far,' murmured Mrs Smith. 'Casey, I'm sorry too. The reason I hid my illness from you – and from myself, I might add – was that I didn't want it to get in the way of everything you've ever dreamed of and worked so hard for. I knew that you'd do what you've done now – drop everything to take care of me. The irony is that in keeping it a secret and not dealing with it, I've made the situation a thousand times worse for both of us. I'm wracked with guilt that I've caused you so much stress and worry at such a crucial point in the season. If I've done irreparable harm to your chances, I'll never forgive myself.'

'Then make it up to me,' implored Casey. 'Teach me again.'

'Casey, I can't. That life is over for me. Thanks to Janet's potion, I feel better this morning than I've done in six months, but you know as well as I do that it's not going to last. No, what I need to do as a matter of urgency is return to Primrose Valley. It's not such a bad place, you know, once you get used to it. The menu leaves a lot to be desired but apart from that ... '

'If that's what you feel you should do then I won't stop you,' Casey said. 'But in that case, would you mind if I borrowed your red notebook? I mean, you won't be needing it at Primrose Valley.'

Mrs Smith tensed. 'Why would you want to do that?'

'I'd like to use it as a training manual for Burghley.'

'Casey, the notes in there are nothing more than the ramblings of an eccentric pensioner.'

'No, they're not. They're brilliant.' Casey cast a cheeky glance at her teacher. 'What's it going to be, Angelica? Do you want to do the sensible thing and return to your room at the hospice, or would you like to do the insane and completely inadvisable thing and join me on a wild quest to do the miraculous? I haven't a hope of winning Burghley without you, you know.'

'Yes, you do. You have the handsome Mr West at your beck and call. You told the *New Equestrian* that leaving me for him was the best decision you ever made. I have to confess I was hurt.'

Casey was shamefaced. 'I don't blame you, but I swear I didn't mean it. It was an idiotic, off-the-cuff comment. Kyle told me to say it and I was still on a high from my win with Roxy so I repeated it. Look, I'm not going to deny that I think Kyle is great. He's a lovely guy and he is, as you say, very handsome, but his methods are not really working for me. If you won't agree to coach me for Burghley then I'm going to withdraw.'

'You wouldn't!'

'Try me.'

'You can't blackmail a sick woman,' said Mrs Smith in a scandalised tone, but there was a twinkle in her eye.

Casey grinned. 'I can and I will, especially if I think that taking on the impossible challenge of the Grand Slam will give you a new lease of life.'

'You're sure about this?'

'I've never been more sure in my life.'

Mrs Smith drew her silk robe more tightly around her thin shoulders. Her voice shook with excitement. 'I'm not going to travel in that horrid lorry, you know.'

'Don't worry, you won't have to. As from next week, the lorry will be no more. Ed Lashley-Jones is taking it away and threatening to sue. You were right about everything. He's spitting mad that I didn't turn up for an Equi-Flow motivational day on Monday – a paintball contest in the New Forest. I was supposed to spend the morning talking about my rags-to-riches rise to Badminton champion and my afternoon crawling through the undergrowth trying to avoid being shot by Equi-Flow clients. I sent Ed a text asking what part of "I have a family emergency" was so hard for him to understand and he took grave offence.'

'He'll get over it,' said Mrs Smith. 'Wendy or Cindi or whatever their names are can mop his fevered brow.'

'So will you do it – teach me?'

Mrs Smith gave her a radiant smile. 'Try stopping me.'

18

CASEY CAUGHT THE train to Wiltshire early next morning. She felt it only fair that she tell Kyle as soon as possible and in person that she would no longer be requiring his services. How he would take it was anybody's guess. Casey had a feeling it wasn't going to go well. She hoped she was wrong because she liked him a great deal and didn't want to upset him, especially after he'd told her his fears about his clients leaving him. But there was too much at stake. She cared about Kyle, but not a fraction as much as she cared about giving Mrs Smith a reason to live.

But as the train sped through the Wiltshire countryside, the image that stuck in her head was of ink dribbling, like blood, down the contract. What if he held her to it? Lawyers would get involved and there could be an ugly and expensive fight to get away from him.

She caught a taxi from the station to Rycliffe Manor. The first time she'd visited, Mr Farley's sat nav had sent them to the rarely used back entrance. The front entrance was much more imposing. Iron gates, flanked by sculpted bronze stallions, glided open as they approached. A sign set into the redbrick wall announced Rycliffe Manor Estate as the 'Proud Home of the Kyle West Equestrian Centre'.

The first person Casey saw when she walked into the yard was Hannah. The junior instructor was sitting on the edge of the fountain reading a thriller. 'Between lessons,' she said in explanation.

Not that Casey had asked. Around the yard she'd heard whispers that Hannah was the least popular of the teachers and struggled to win clients. Casey couldn't understand why, although she could see that Hannah had a jealous streak. Madly in love with her boss, Hannah's attitude towards her had gone from lukewarm to extra frosty as Kyle's interest in Casey had increased and her supposed boyfriend had failed to put in an appearance at Rycliffe Manor.

'If it's Kyle you're after you'll have a long wait,' Hannah said pointedly now. 'He's with an important client.'

Casey did a mental eye roll. Mr Farley would be arriving with the lorry at any moment and she wanted to speak to Kyle and be on her way with Storm as soon as she could. But she wasn't about to confide in Hannah.

'No problem. I'll wait for him in the office.' She was dying to see her beloved horse, but she wanted to get the Kyle speech over first.

She was halfway to the cool stone building that housed the video suite, office and guest quarters when she remembered Anna Sparks' words. Turning suddenly, she was startled to catch Hannah staring after her, a peculiar expression on her face.

'Everything all right, Hannah?'

'What? Oh, yes. I was miles away. I was thinking about the plot of my novel. It's a murder mystery set in a racing stable.' She shoved the novel into her bag as if that would make it less scary. 'Did you want something?'

'Who's Mouse? A friend of mine mentioned that he used to come here.'

Hannah laughed. 'That's one way of putting it. Mouse was the stable name of Anna Sparks' horse. You remember, the one she drove mad – Rough Diamond.'

Casey thanked her and hurried away to the office before Hannah could ask any awkward questions about which friend had talked to her about Mouse. She was in turmoil. The majority of people who'd witnessed Anna's attack on Best Man at Badminton would be of the same view as Hannah – that if anyone was to blame for Rough Diamond's breakdown it was Anna Sparks herself.

Yet at Aston-le-Walls, Anna had claimed that Rough Diamond was never the same again after what 'they' did to him. Did 'they' mean Kyle and Ray or someone else altogether?

Casey slowed as she reached the office. Joyce was on the phone, arguing with someone over the non-payment of a bill. She didn't notice Casey start up the stairs.

On the landing, Casey paused. She needed to pull herself together and formulate a plan. In the conversation she'd overheard, Kyle had snapped: 'The way it worked with Mouse, you mean?'

'That wasn't my fault,' was Ray's snarled response. 'The girl was out of control.'

Was the girl in question Anna Sparks? If so, who had been responsible for harming her horse?

More urgently, where was Storm? Was he okay?

A voice cut into her thoughts. The door of the video suite was open and she could hear Ray talking in a low, urgent tone. Casey crept up the final few steps. If Ray was on the phone perhaps she could get a sense of the man behind the mask.

But as she approached the door, she saw that he wasn't chatting to some remote caller at all. He was speaking into a microphone. On the television monitor before him an elegant woman was schooling a horse.

'If she wants her horse to lengthen his stride during the trot, she needs to drive him forward so that she has a more consistent connection. His ribcage will feel a lot looser,' he was saying.

There was a crackle as Kyle's disembodied voice relayed the instruction to the rider as if it was coming from him.

'That's better,' Ray said into the microphone, 'but

remind her to keep leaning on the inside of her stirrup. The more she does that, the closer she'll be to her horse's centre of gravity. That's the final tip. Lesson's over.'

'Okay, Steph, we're done for the day,' said Kyle. 'Keep leaning on the inside of your stirrups. It'll keep you nearer to your horse's sense of gravity.'

Casey felt as if she had fallen into a shaft with no bottom. The whole operation was a scam. Every last bit of it. Kyle was the suave, charismatic front for the centre. He was customer- and media-friendly and looked good gracing the covers of magazines. Ray was the expert, but he was not a people person. His battered face and surly manner gave the wrong impression. Worse still, he had contempt for the clients. He made it obvious that he knew far more about their horses than they did.

In that instant Casey was certain that whatever had happened to Rough Diamond was Ray's fault. Kyle had been involved in the deception of the riders, but it was clear that Ray alone manipulated the horses.

Casey began to shiver. If they were capable of a deception on this grand a scale, what else were they capable of? She had to get Storm away from here.

Her mobile beeped. Mr Farley had arrived with the lorry. She grabbed her phone to silence it, but it was too late. Ray was at the door. He knew immediately that she'd seen and heard everything. Reacting with a boxer's speed, he barred her escape route, fists clenched at his side. 'If you breathe a word about this, you'll be sorry.'

From far away, Casey heard Kyle's voice in the office

downstairs. He was saying something to Joyce. Ray stepped back and folded his arms.

Kyle came rushing up the steps, his face alight. 'Hey, Casey, Joyce said you were back. Sorry to keep you waiting.'

He stopped when he saw her expression.

'What's going on?'

'Casey knows everything,' said Ray. 'She heard me talk you through the lesson.'

Kyle covered his face with his hands. 'No.' When he lifted his head, Casey saw again the little boy that lived inside him. 'Casey, I can explain. It's not what it looks like. I—'

'Save it,' snapped Ray. 'This is not something you can sweet talk your way out of, Kyle. The game is up. But don't worry. She's not going to tell anyone, are you, Casey? Not if she wants to get to Burghley in one piece.'

'Don't you dare threaten her,' yelled Kyle.

'Or what? What will you do about it? I told you that you were making a mistake choosing this girl. I told you it was a bridge too far. It was obvious you were half in love with her before you even met her. I told you that you'd ruin everything if you didn't get your emotions under control.'

'And I told you that by trying to live your dreams through me you'd destroy my life. Congratulations. That's what you've done. Well, it's over. You and I and this whole charade, it's over.'

For a second the two men's faces were in profile and

that's when it clicked. Casey gasped. 'Now I get it. You're father and son.'

Ray gave a short laugh. 'I wondered how long it would take for someone to cotton on. Incredibly, you're the first to figure it out. That's what happens when you're the ugly father of a beautiful son. People don't make the connection. Kyle takes after his mother, you see.'

'But why the secrecy? Who cares if you're related?'

Ray glanced at Kyle, who was slumped against the wall. He opened his mouth as if to say something then thought better of it. 'Seemed better that way.'

Picking up his car keys, he gave Casey a warning look. 'Remember what I said. Mind you watch your mouth.'

As his footsteps faded, Kyle jerked to life like a statue becoming real. 'Casey, I don't know what to say.'

'Don't bother saying anything, Kyle. I'm going to get my horse and go. I'm not interested in your excuses or your lies. Oh, and don't worry, I won't be telling anyone. Just leave me and Storm alone. You owe us that much.'

She flew down the stairs and out into the yard, almost knocking over Hannah, who'd heard shouting and come to investigate. When she reached Storm's stable and saw that he was leaning over his door, ears pricked, whickering with joy at the sight of her, she could have wept with relief. With shaking hands, she put on his headcollar and rug.

'We're going home,' she told him. 'You're safe now and we're going home.'

Never had she been so happy to see the monosyllabic

Mr Farley. As quickly as she could, she loaded Storm and ran back to the tack room to collect her saddle and bridle. She was hunting for her girth when Kyle appeared in the doorway.

He looked so utterly crushed, his handsome face drawn, that Casey's heart went out to him. She hardened it at once, but he'd seen her weaken and was already moving forward.

'Casey, there's nothing I can do or say to make up for what's happened. Believe me, I feel like the lowest person on earth. But I couldn't let you go without some explanation. The whole coaching thing, it was Dad's dream. I—'

'Oh, so it's Dad now, is it? Not Ray. You told me your father was dead, Kyle. In the grave. How could you lie about something like that?'

He reddened. 'It's a long story. You see, Dad – Ray – always had a gift for working with horses and riders. As a young man his goal was to teach the top horsemen in every discipline, but although he achieved phenomenal results he was always passed over in favour of teachers with a fraction of his talent. Because he looks and sometimes talks like a prize fighter, no one ever took him seriously. It frustrated him so much that he became bitter and angry. Like your father, he made a series of terrible decisions and we all had to suffer the consequences.

'One day it occurred to me that I could make him proud and at the same time make up for some of his disappointments if I became an instructor myself. It wasn't what I wanted to do with my life, but I love horses so I thought it would be easy. I enrolled on an instructor course. Within days it was obvious that I was hopeless.'

'So you came up with a plan to combine your talents?'

'It was Dad's idea. He convinced me to try it for an exam. It was so easy and worked so well that he became obsessed with doing it for real. I was reluctant to go along with it at first. I was sure that we'd be caught and the fallout would be horrific. But somehow we never were. Money started pouring in and reporters started writing about me and before I knew it the whole thing had snowballed out of control. Initially I was eaten up with guilt, but I justified it as a short-term solution. I persuaded myself that as soon as I'd learned as much as Ray, I'd be able to teach on my own. But it didn't work out that way. The more successful I became, the more pressure I was under to be this miracle-working guru. I didn't dare tell riders like you my own theories in case I was exposed as a fraud. Every day I felt as if I was walking a tightrope without a safety net.'

'But that first day at White Oaks. How did you know what to say to me then?'

'Some of it was improvised. I've watched Ray deal with biting horses for years, for example, so that part was easy. Some of it he'd told me to say in advance. He'd watched you ride at Badminton so he had a few theories that applied in any situation. Casey, I'm sorry.

More sorry than you can possibly imagine. Things just snowballed. They got out of hand.'

Casey spotted the girth hanging over a different saddle and snatched it up.

'I'd like to sympathise with you, Kyle, but right now I'm shattered. You and your dad – what you've done is fraud. I trusted you, Kyle. *You.* Not Ray. Most alarmingly, I trusted you with Storm and my career. Never in a million years would I have willingly put either my horse or my future in the hands of Ray. Don't compare him to my dad. My father is a caring, decent man. He's not perfect but he would never, ever harm an animal. How could you let Ray ruin Rough Diamond?'

She stared him in the eye, willing him to tell the truth. 'It was Ray, wasn't it? Anna got the blame but it was your dad's fault.'

Kyle was grey with misery. 'He didn't ... I wasn't sure ... Anna was behaving like a princess and someone had to take control. Ray understands horses. He said that Mouse was too arrogant and that he'd perform better if he was made to understand who was in charge ... '

All of a sudden Casey felt exhausted beyond words. 'I think I've heard enough. I'm going. Storm's already loaded and I need to get him home.'

She moved to get the saddle, but Kyle grabbed her arm. 'Casey, wait. Please don't end it like this. Don't you understand that the reason I'm so devastated is because it's you I've betrayed? I love you. I think I've loved you from the moment I saw you ride at Badminton. Don't tell me you feel nothing for me because I won't believe you.'

Before Casey could move or resist he kissed her.

A shadow fell across the doorway. 'Now I see why you haven't been returning my calls.'

Casey tore her lips from Kyle's and sprang back. Peter was staring at her in horror.

'I heard about Mrs Smith and came as soon as I could, but nobody seemed to know where you were. Finally, I got hold of your father and he told me you were on your way to Rycliffe Manor. I was reluctant to come here but I thought you might need me. I guess I was wrong. You've found a different shoulder to cry on.'

Without another word, he strode away across the yard.

Casey gave Kyle a furious glare. 'Now look what you've done.'

She sprinted after Peter, but when she reached the car park his van was already halfway across the estate. The love of her life had gone.

19

ON A STIFLINGLY warm afternoon in mid-August Angelica Smith sat in a deckchair and watched Casey work with Storm. By her calculation the silver horse was a couple of weeks away from reaching prime condition, but then hers was the opinion of a perfectionist. To a casual observer, he was a majestic sight, a virtual equine machine. His break from competition had done him a power of good, as had the intense fitness regime of the past few weeks, especially the steeplechasing. He was hungry again, burning to gallop and jump.

Casey was a different matter. On the one hand, her work ethic could not be faulted. She was completely focused on getting herself and Storm in the best possible shape for the Burghley Horse Trials in the third week of

September, less than a month away. The bad habits that had crept in while she and Mrs Smith had been 'on a break' (that was how they jokingly referred to their time apart) had been jettisoned. No more lying on the sofa eating microwaved pizza or takeaway chips. No more chocolate or multiple cappuccinos. Nothing but raw egg, yogurt and spirulina smoothies and wholesome vegetarian cooking with lots of brown rice.

To anyone who didn't know her, Casey looked incredible. Her dark hair was thick and glossy and her grey eyes clear and bright. Her enviably tanned slender limbs were those of a professional athlete. But those were all physical things. Psychologically, she was lower than Mrs Smith had ever seen her. Peter had returned to Ireland and was refusing to take her calls. She was putting on a brave front but Mrs Smith knew a broken heart when she saw one.

'The worst thing about it is I brought it on myself,' Casey had said in their only conversation on the subject. 'I never stopped loving Peter, but I allowed myself to be seduced by Kyle's looks and the whole glamorous package that came with him – the sports car, the beautiful estate, the sophisticated parties. I can't blame Kyle if he thought I was flirting with him. At times, maybe I was. And now I've lost the best thing that ever happened to me.'

'Give Peter space,' Mrs Smith had counselled. 'He's wounded but he'll come round.'

Privately she wasn't so sure. Peter was passionately in love with Casey but he had a stubborn streak. He also had a strong sense of right and wrong. If he thought she'd cheated on him, he wouldn't easily be won over.

As Casey transitioned to a walk Mrs Smith called out: 'Storm had too much bend in his neck during the shoulder-in. On the next corner I want you to let him think he is going into the diagonal but ask him to shoulder-in down the long side instead.'

Shortly afterwards she waved for her pupil to come in. They'd been training hard for forty-five minutes and Mrs Smith didn't believe in pushing a horse any harder. There was nothing to be gained from turning Storm sour.

Casey's skin had a fine sheen of sweat, but neither she nor Storm was remotely puffed as they came to a halt. 'It's working, isn't it?' she said excitedly. 'Your red notebook plan; it's doing everything we hoped it would.'

Mrs Smith had been so close to death at Primrose Valley that she now felt as if she could actually taste life. To her, every extra hour was a gift, not merely because she was alive but because she was with Casey and Storm, doing what she loved. That the red notebook plan was indeed working was a bonus.

'I can't take all the credit,' Mrs Smith said modestly.

Casey laughed as she slid off Storm and rewarded him with Polo mints. 'I know, I know, it was Lucinda Green, six times Badminton champion. She's the one who sowed the seeds of your brilliant strategy.'

Mrs Smith handed her a bottle of water and poured herself a mug of chai from a flask. 'It's true, she did.

It was a comment she made when we had a brief conversation during the Kentucky Three-Day Event. We were discussing the Grand Slam and why no one but Pippa Funnell has won it. Lucinda felt that Burghley presented a unique set of challenges because the ground was extremely undulating. In terms of terrain, it's far tougher than Badminton and the Kentucky Three-Day Event. That's why horses that train on all-weather surfaces are the ones who suffer most in terms of exhaustion. To her, the key is to get a horse fit on as many types of terrain as possible.'

Casey undid Storm's girth and took off his saddle. 'Is that how you got onto the subject of the long format of eventing versus the short format?'

'Basically, yes. Like a lot of people, Lucinda feels that since the FEI did away with the roads and tracks and steeplechase section of four-star events, horses aren't as fit as they used to be. I agree. A tired horse is a horse that can misjudge a fence. And when you're riding one of the most treacherous cross-country courses in the world, the smallest error can lead to disaster.

'It doesn't help that the format of CCI four-star events means that you go from the sedateness of dressage to the speed and high risk of the cross-country. Previously, you had the roads and tracks and steeplechase phase in between to get a horse thinking. Research shows that there were fewer rotational falls in those days because the long format took the edge off the energy of the hottest horses and enabled them to arrive at the cross-country with their mind on the job. There are also statistics showing that it led to fewer stress-related injuries such as bowed tendons.'

Casey turned on the hose and ran cool water over Storm. He wrinkled his muzzle as she washed his head and neck. 'So you thought you'd adapt the format to suit Storm and me?'

'Exactly. The long format takes too much out of the horse. The short format is too short. So I thought we might do something in between. In our training, we'll include the steeplechase, as we've been doing for the past few weeks. But on cross-country day at Burghley, we'll only do roads and tracks – perhaps with a few hedges and other natural obstacles added in. I've spoken to the farmer who owns the land adjacent to Burghley Park. He has no problem with us using his farm as an extension of the cross-country course.'

Casey switched off the water. 'Are we really doing this, Angelica? Are we really going to attempt the impossible?'

Mrs Smith's heart skipped a beat. 'Yes, Casey, we really are.'

20

THAT EVENING, CASEY made them both a vegetarian cottage pie topped with liberal quantities of grated cheddar. Mrs Smith was the better cook, but Casey was determined to ease her workload. She'd arranged for a cleaner to come twice a week and insisted on doing all the shopping and chores herself.

Ignoring her teacher's protests, she'd also insisted on having a legal agreement drawn up making Mrs Smith her manager.

'There's no point. I don't know how long I'll be around.'

'I don't care if you're here for one day or ten years,' said Casey. 'Well, I do, but you know what I mean. I want you protected and I want you to know that, along with Peter and my dad, you're the most important person in my life. You're family to me. You're something more than that too. You're my mentor and my best friend. Anything I've ever achieved or ever will achieve is because of you.'

'Thank you, Casey. That's quite enough compliments to be going on with,' Mrs Smith said sternly. Praise always made her uncomfortable. 'You might want to check on the cottage pie. There's smoke pouring out of the oven.'

As Casey raced to rescue the dinner, Mrs Smith watched her with a smile. It was good to have the old Casey back, and fairly wonderful to be back herself. Thanks to Janet's special potion and Mr Mutandwa's painkillers, she felt better than she'd done in months. She could function. She could walk and think and she had hope.

Janet's magic mix had come with only one condition.

'This concoction is packed full of stimulants to keep you going, but in your fragile state I can't vouch for the consequences. Will you promise me that you won't exert yourself too much or do anything that radically raises your heart rate? Keep calm and don't do anything silly.'

Mrs Smith had laughed. 'Janet, my dear, I think my aerobic days are behind me. I don't think I've jogged anywhere since I ran a five kilometre race for charity in my forties. Have no worries on that score.'

As Casey scraped the burned bits off the cottage pie, Mrs Smith sat at the kitchen table deep in thought. Knowing that she'd never breathe a word, Casey had confided to her every detail of the Rycliffe Manor scam.

The problem was what to do about it. What Kyle and Ray had done was not a crime. At worst, they were guilty of misrepresentation. And Kyle had said he would no longer be part of the charade. Nothing good could come of exposing them.

They couldn't even warn other riders on the circuit – people like Sam Tide, the Australian rider, one of Kyle's star clients, in case there were repercussions. Despite Ray's threat, Casey was convinced that he would never risk actually harming her, but she was afraid that he would find a way to get to Storm.

Mrs Smith, however, was not one to do nothing in the face of injustice. Casey's description of the dog attack had chilled her to the marrow. She was certain that it had somehow been engineered, probably by the sinister Ray. She was equally sure that anyone capable of such a heinous act had done similar things – or worse – before. With that in mind, she'd contacted Detective Inspector Lenny McLeod, the policeman who'd helped Casey deal with a blackmailer a few months before.

McLeod owned a Morgan mare and was officially horse mad. Having read dozens of articles on Kyle West, he was surprised when Mrs Smith asked him, in confidence and as a friend, to run a background check on Ray Cook, manager of the Rycliffe Manor Equestrian Centre. Three days later he rang her with the results. Ray's record was squeaky clean.

'Not even a parking ticket,' he told her. 'Why, what were you expecting me to find?'

'I'm not sure. I suppose I was mistaken. Thanks for looking into it.'

'No problem. There are a couple of other searches I could try. If I find anything I'll let you know.'

Casey set a plate in front of Mrs Smith. 'One gourmet serving of chargrilled cottage pie. Jamie Oliver eat your heart out.'

As she sat down her phone rang. 'Mind if I get it?'

Mrs Smith shook her head. She knew that Casey was hoping it was Peter.

The voice on the end was confident and well-spoken. 'Casey Blue? This is Casper Leyton. You attended one of my parties a while back.'

Casey was thrown. 'Uh, yes, Mr Leyton. Thank you. It was kind of you to invite me. I had a great time.' Raising her eyebrows at Mrs Smith, she put him on speakerphone.

'Call me Casper. Casey, I have a proposition for you. I have a four-star horse named Incendiary who is on form and more than capable of winning the Burghley Horse Trials. That's not just my opinion. That's the verdict of some of the best experts in the business. His pedigree has to be seen to be believed. He's been competing in New Zealand this season and has blown everything out of the water. Mark Todd tried to buy him but I got in first. I was hoping to persuade a friend of mine to ride him at Burghley but it turns out that he has already entered another two horses. He recommended I ring you.

'I'll be truthful, my initial response was that you were

far too young. But your track record is impressive. Added to which if you pull off a miracle and make history, it would give my business the kind of publicity boost that money can't buy. So how about it? Fancy a second ride? It would give a massive boost to your chances.'

Casey was reeling. Many of the top riders rode one or more horses at four-star events for the simple reason that it doubled or tripled their chances of grabbing eventing's most glittering prizes. If the first horse performed poorly or was injured, there was always the hope that the other would save the day. If Incendiary was as good as Casper claimed he was Casey's chances of winning the Grand Slam would increase dramatically.

'I'm flattered that you'd consider me, Mr Leyton. I – well, I'm not quite sure how to respond. Thank you. It's an amazing offer. Would it be okay if I discussed it with my coach before giving you an answer?'

'Kyle West?'

'Angelica Smith is now my teacher.'

'Oh.' There was a pause. 'Sure. Take as long as you need. Write down my number. Give me a ring when you've made up your mind.'

Casey clicked off the phone and looked across the table at Mrs Smith. 'What do you think?'

'I think that it's a decision only you can make. What I can tell you is that I read an article on Incendiary a couple of months ago and he's the real deal. If God designed an event horse, it would be him. His conformation and balance are quite exceptional. If you rode well, you'd be in pole position for the title. Of course, you might have to accept that the horse that helped you get there isn't Storm Warning. Storm is a champion and the bravest horse I've ever known, but Incendiary is in a different league.'

She covered Casey's hand with hers. 'Do what feels right, my dear. I'll support you either way.'

Casey nodded slowly. She tapped in Casper's number. He answered before it rang.

'That was quick. So what's it going to be? Are we going to go for the Slam together?'

'Mr Leyton, I can't thank you enough for giving me this opportunity. To be honest, I'm blown away by it. But I'm going to have to turn it down.'

'Turn it down?! Am I hearing you correctly? Maybe I haven't done a good enough job of explaining that this is the chance of a lifetime.' Casper Leyton was unaccustomed to taking no for an answer.

'Please don't think that I'm in any way ungrateful. I just don't feel that I'm the right rider for your horse. If he's as special as you say he is, you need a rider who is dedicated to Incendiary alone and not someone with divided loyalties, as I would have with Storm. I hope you understand.'

Casper Leyton gave a grudging laugh. 'I don't, but I appreciate your frankness and I admire your devotion to your horse. Doesn't mean that I think you're any less crazy for turning mine down, but I respect your decision. If that's your final word on the matter, I should tell you that there is another rider in the frame. You were my first choice, but I'm going to move to Plan B and you're not going to like it.'

'I doubt I'll have an opinion. Who you choose to ride your horse is your own business.'

'From what I hear, you will have an opinion about this rider. I'm going to give Incendiary to Anna Sparks.'

Casey almost dropped the phone. 'Anna Sparks? But ... but ...'

'That's the reaction I've had from everyone. "Anna Sparks...!" Cue stammering and apoplexy. My own advisors think I've lost my mind. I know she's a risk but it's a risk I am prepared to take. It is true that she lost her temper at Badminton and lashed out at Best Man, but if you watch the video on YouTube, you'll see that she only once made contact with him. Most of the time she was just hitting out in a blind rage.'

'And that makes it okay?'

'No, but I'm confident Anna is no longer the same person. She's learned some painful lessons. She's lost every friend and every sponsor and been pilloried by the newspapers. She's changed. People do. If she's guilty of anything it's of letting fame go to her head. Speaking from experience, she's not alone.'

'No,' Casey said, 'she's not.'

'Everyone deserves a second chance,' said Casper Leyton.

After he'd hung up, Casey switched off her phone and picked up her fork. Her cottage pie was cold.

Mrs Smith was watching her in puzzlement. 'When Leyton told you he was giving the horse to Anna Sparks, why didn't you change your mind? You could have stopped him. This is a girl who, only a few months ago, behaved monstrously towards you. She was your sworn enemy. Now you've handed her the ride of a lifetime. It could mean the difference between you winning or losing.'

21

THREE-DAY EVENTING first became a recognised sport at the Olympic Games in Stockholm in 1912. Its governing body, the Fédération Equestre Internationale (FEI) describes this multidisciplinary competition as one in which the aim is to 'show the rider's spirit, boldness and perfect knowledge of his horse's paces and their use across country, and to show the condition, handiness, courage, jumping ability, stamina, and speed of the well-trained horse.'

In the days when riding so much as a gymkhana on the intransigent Patchwork seemed like reaching for the stars, Casey had committed this passage to memory. It came back to her now, in a nostalgic wave, as she crossed the courtyard to Burghley House for the annual

Thursday night riders and owners cocktail party.

In the driveway outside, the most famous names in horse trials were alighting from SUVs and sports cars in tuxedos, evening gowns and little black dresses. Since eventing requires a degree of physical fitness unheard of outside horse racing, most looked like models or film stars, but it was odd to see them out of their riding gear. Like Casey, most preferred breeches and boots.

Walking in alone in her short black dress and high heels – bought for Casper Leyton's party – Casey felt like Cinderella wrongly invited to the ball. Then Marsha joined her, which was worse. Casey had decided she didn't particularly like Sam Tide's groom, who was only at Burghley House because she'd again posed as Sam's date. Unless they were wealthy and made regular appearances in *Tatler*, *Vogue* or *Horse & Hound*, Marsha seldom had a good word to say about anyone.

'It just goes to show that money doesn't buy common sense,' Marsha was saying as she sipped at a blue cocktail with a cherry floating in it. 'Casper Leyton must have a screw loose. Why else would he allow a dangerous lunatic like Anna Sparks to ride a horse like Incendiary at Burghley? Sam is livid. He could have done with a second ride. Obviously, he'll be one of the favourites to win here no matter what, but Incendiary would pretty much have guaranteed that he'd walk away with the title. Depending, of course, on Michael Jung. One can never rule him out.'

She fished the cherry out of her drink and crunched

it up. Interestingly, it didn't occur to her to include Casey and Storm among the list of potential winners. It shouldn't have mattered but Casey was irritated by the omission.

'You can blame me,' she told Marsha. 'It was because I turned Incendiary down that Casper decided to offer the horse to Anna.'

Marsha almost spat out the remains of the cherry. 'Come again? You did what? Are you mental?'

'I'm not sure. Probably. Sam already has a horse to ride at Burghley. Anna will be focused on Incendiary and she'll give it everything she's got.'

The expression on Marsha's face as Casey walked off was well worth the sleepless nights Casey had had since reading an outraged editorial in the *New Equestrian* about Casper Leyton's controversial decision to hire eventing's *enfant terrible* to ride his horse at Burghley.

And what a horse Incendiary was. Casey had seen the stallion for the first time earlier that afternoon. He was the colour of Mocha coffee with muscles that coiled and rippled beneath his satin hide. But the most striking thing about him was his balance. As Anna transitioned from a canter to a medium trot, he seemed to float like a mythical being. Watching him, Casey knew immediately that she'd made a potentially catastrophic miscalculation. If Anna was at the top of her game, the pair would be a significant threat.

Still, Casey didn't regret doing what she'd done. It was Storm's courage and power that had carried her to

214

victory at Badminton and Kentucky. If she was fortunate enough to have glory come her way at Burghley, she wanted it only if Storm was part of it and could share in it. The idea of riding a horse that might beat him was intolerable.

Casey had been about to return to the lorry park when Anna came after her. 'Casey, wait, please. I need to speak to you.' Pulling up the stallion, she patted him delightedly before dismounting.

'Isn't he the most heavenly creature on earth? Well, he is to me anyway. I suppose you feel the same about Storm Warning. Casey, I can't begin to thank you. Casper told me that it was only because you didn't want to ride any other horse but Storm that he hired me. Casper's read me the riot act, of course. If I damage so much as a hair on Incendiary's head I might as well emigrate to Brazil.'

'Then don't,' Casey said. 'Treat him like gold.'

'Oh, I will.'

Casey studied Incendiary. He seemed relaxed and kept nuzzling Anna's pockets for treats – surely a positive sign. 'Have a good Burghley, Anna. See you on the other side.'

'Same to you. See you on the other side.'

At the cocktail party, Casey left Marsha looking thunderstruck and retreated to a corner of the room where she felt less exposed. Along the way, people patted her on the back and wished her luck for the championship. Casey found a shadowed spot and stood there nursing a glass of elderflower. She wished she hadn't come. The face she most wanted to see was absent. As a farrier, Peter hadn't been invited. Even if he had been, he wouldn't have come. A cocktail party in a stately home wasn't him at all.

Casey checked her watch. Very shortly she'd make her excuses and return to the hired lorry where Mrs Smith was waiting. She only had to make it through another ten minutes.

Peter was at that moment checking Incendiary's shoes. Casper Leyton had asked him to fit them the previous week. It was at Leyton's stables that he'd learned that Casey had refused the offer of the stallion out of loyalty to Storm.

Peter had been thrown by this news. It had forced him to revise his opinion that Casey was no longer the girl with whom he'd fallen in love, but it still wasn't enough to make him call her. He'd caught her red-handed with Kyle. Who knew how many times it had happened before? She'd not only broken his heart, she'd trampled on it, and he wanted nothing more to do with her.

On his return to Ireland, he'd gone out of his way to

kiss Orla at the first opportunity. It had only happened the once because he found that kissing someone other than his girlfriend had nauseated him. He realised then that he loved Casey in a way that was infinite. If he moved to the ends of the earth, she'd still inhabit his whole heart and soul. She'd ruined him for every other girl.

As if that weren't bad enough, he'd misjudged Orla. Sucked in by her beauty and ample charms, he had been appalled to discover, on the last day of his course, that she'd hidden his phone beneath the cupboard in his room. He couldn't prove it was her but he knew it was. On it were at least a dozen missed calls, texts and messages from Casey. It was some consolation but it wasn't enough. Nothing could make up for the agony he'd felt when he saw her kissing Kyle.

'How do they look?'

He stood up. Anna Sparks was in the doorway, wearing jeans and a polo-shirt. He almost didn't recognise her. She'd cut her hair and put on weight and bore no resemblance to the princess who'd once ruled the circuit. In Peter's opinion her new look was an improvement but then he'd never liked over-made-up fashion victims.

'His feet are perfect. How has he ridden since I shod him? Any tenderness?'

'None at all. His paces are fantastic. Lighter than air. Thank you, Peter. You've done a brilliant job, as usual.'

Peter stared at her in astonishment. In all the years he and his father had spent shoeing the Sparks' horses, he didn't ever recall the word thanks leaving Anna's mouth. She and her ghastly friend 'V,' a girl conspicuous now by her absence, had spent most of their time making fun of him.

'You're welcome. How are you? Not going to the cocktail party with the other riders?'

There was a split-second of hesitation before she responded: 'Not this year. I wanted to check on Incendiary and go over my test for tomorrow's dressage. How about you? Why aren't you with Casey?'

'We broke up,' Peter blurted out before he could stop himself.

She circled Incendiary and nodded approvingly at his new shoes before answering. 'It's none of my business, but are you nuts? The two of you are made for each other.'

'You're right. It's none of your business. But if you must know, she prefers someone else.'

'I don't believe you,' said Anna. 'Who is this person she supposedly prefers? Is it a rider? If you're talking about Kyle West, you're barking up the wrong tree. Kyle is every girl's dream man—'

'Thanks!'

'Can I finish my sentence? He's every girl's dream in terms of looks, but he has issues. I don't want to get into it, but there are armies of ghosts in his past. Something to do with his dead father. To make up for it, Kyle has this overwhelming need to make everybody love him. He did it with me and Casey wouldn't have been any different.'

'If you're trying to make me feel worse than I already do, you're doing a great job.'

'Anna gave an exasperated sigh. 'Will you be patient and let me finish? I was going to say that whatever feelings he may or may not have had for her, they weren't returned. My father's former business partner owns Rycliffe Manor. He called me recently about something to do with my dad. We got onto the subject of the equestrian centre and he told me that Casey ran out after a blazing row with Kyle about six weeks ago and they haven't spoken since.'

Hope flickered in Peter's heart. 'How do you know they haven't been in contact?'

'Because Kyle left the country on some undisclosed mission at around the same time. For all I know, he might still be abroad. Ray has been teaching all his clients. They were furious at first, especially Sam Tide, but now they've decided that he's even better than Kyle. He's an oddball and his methods are unusual but he does know horses inside out. Or at least he thinks he does. Personally, I think that the two of them ruin as many horses as they fix, but I'm not sure that anyone apart from Casey would share that view.'

'Why are you telling me this, Anna?'

'Because I owe Casey. Don't be a muppet, Peter. Casey worships the ground you walk on. Go to her before the championship starts and make her smile.'

'I don't know. I'll have to think about it.'

With a flash of her old imperiousness, Anna said:

'Peter Rhys, are you honestly saying that you've never made a mistake in your life?'

Peter went crimson.

Anna rolled her eyes. 'Exactly.'

After she'd gone, Peter leaned against the stable door. He felt oddly exhilarated. Anna was right. If he didn't fight for the girl he loved, he'd regret it for the rest of his life.

But how could he get to her? She was at the cocktail party at Burghley House. Later, she'd join the other riders at the members' enclosure dinner. She'd be surrounded by admirers. He had no invitation to either event, nor did he have the right clothes. Faded black jeans and a creased denim shirt with a missing button hardly qualified as correct dress for a black tie party. If he went bursting into Burghley House like a lovelorn character in a film, people would fall down laughing.

No, he'd have to wait until after Casey had finished her dressage test on Friday and try to find the right time to approach her then.

He was about to leave the stables when it occurred to him that there was one thing he could do for Casey that evening. He could check Storm's feet. If there were any shoeing problems that might hamper the horse in the dressage, he could secretly put them right.

Peter started in the direction of the block where Storm was stabled. As he approached he thought he saw a shadow move. Seconds later, a door banged shut. Peter quickened his pace. There'd been break-ins and horse tampering at other events in the past. Burghley had superb security, but one never knew. It only took a second.

When he reached Storm's stable, he was relieved to see the horse munching on his hay net. Rarely had he looked better. His silver coat had a mercurial gleam and his condition was superb.

'Hello, champ. How's it going?'

Peter let himself in and Storm whickered with pleasure. He was pining for Casey and Roxy, but his favourite farrier was a welcome substitute. Lifting his feet happily, he allowed Peter to examine his shoes.

A door squeaked open and heels came tip-tapping along the corridor. Storm's ears pricked.

'Hello, gorgeous,' said Casey. 'Couldn't stay away. I was missing you.'

She didn't notice Peter until he stepped out from behind Storm and gave her a lingering look that took in every detail of her sexy black dress, long, shapely legs and the dark hair she'd tried unsuccessfully to tame.

'That's good to hear,' he said with a grin, 'because I've missed you too.'

22

CASEY PULLED HER long black boots over breeches as white as fresh snow and zipped them up. Thanks to Mrs Smith, they'd been polished to a military shine. Over her white shirt, she put her navy-blue coat and tails, hand-stitched for her by her father, now a qualified tailor. On the cuffs he'd embroidered a delicate rose design. It was a tribute to her mum, as was the rose brooch Casey carried in her pocket. Having it with her always made Casey feel as if her mother was riding with her like a guardian angel, sharing in every high and low.

Unlike the Equi-Flow lorry, the back of the hired one was cramped, but Casey didn't mind in the least. This one came without strings attached. Opening the narrow closet, she checked herself in the mirror. She looked a lot more poised than she felt.

In under an hour she would be competing for the ultimate prize in eventing. It was hard to take in. Many experts were of the opinion that the Burghley Horse Trials had taken over from Badminton as the toughest Three-Day Event in the world. If she won ...

But, no, Mrs Smith had told her to put both victory and the Grand Slam completely out of her mind. As far as she was concerned, Casey had enough on her plate without ratcheting up the pressure even further. Casey was inclined to agree. Today was about posting a decent dressage result, nothing more, nothing less.

Putting her top hat over her short, neatly gelled dark hair, Casey stepped out of the lorry. Mrs Smith and Peter were waiting with her horse. Storm's head went up and his ears pricked when he saw her. Nothing got his blood racing like competition. He pranced on the spot, showing off. Mrs Smith, who'd had rather more sleep than Casey, had insisted on plaiting his mane. Needless to say, his turnout was of Grand Prix quality.

Casey felt a rush of love when she saw him. In a way, it was because of Storm that she and Peter were back together. There'd been no dramatic scenes. As soon as they saw one another, they'd rushed to embrace.

When at last they separated, Casey said, 'Peter, I'm so sorry about what happened with Kyle. It really wasn't what you thought. He—'

Peter put a finger to her lips. 'Stop. I'm sorry too. I'm

no good at being away from you. I hate it. I want to always be with you. If you'll have me, that is.'

'Oh, I'll have you,' Casey responded cheekily.

There'd been chemistry between her and Kyle, but like everything else it was based on an illusion. When he kissed her, she'd felt only guilt. Peter's kisses sent an electrical storm crackling through her veins. As he held her to him, they fitted together. There was a rightness about Peter that went to her core.

Putting her arms around his waist, she looked up at him. 'Wish me luck in the dressage?'

'I do, but you won't need it.' Leaning down he whispered: 'You look devastatingly beautiful, by the way.'

Turning to Mrs Smith, Casey held out her hands. Her teacher gripped them. 'Just do your best, my dear. Nothing else matters.'

Casey's eyes were suddenly bright with emotion. 'Thank you for everything and especially for being here.'

'Wouldn't miss it for the world. I love you, Casey, and I'm more proud of you than you'll ever know.'

'Love you too.'

As Casey swung onto Storm, boosted by Peter, Detective Inspector Lenny McLeod hurried up. He'd been on a health kick since she'd last seen him and was almost unrecognisable as the podgy policeman who'd accompanied Peter to Kentucky. He'd traded caffeine, fast food and lonely all-nighters for the gym and more days out with his Morgan mare, Montana. It suited him.

His grey hair was neatly trimmed and he was fit and slim in his plain clothes – a white shirt, grey blazer and jeans.

The only thing that hadn't changed was his razor-sharp gaze. It raked the faces of the passing crowd like a scimitar, daring them to commit a crime and get away with it. Casey could imagine it acting as a truth serum on any criminal who stood before him.

McLeod was at the championship as a friend, but also on unofficial business. After Mrs Smith's phone call about Ray Cook, he had done some investigating into the staff at Rycliffe Manor. He knew that she'd never have contacted him unless she had serious cause for suspicion. While he'd found no specific evidence of wrongdoing, there was enough smoke for him to be convinced that a fire was either about to start or already smouldering. One person in particular had a background that set all sorts of alarm bells ringing. Gut instinct had driven him to Burghley. He saw no harm in keeping a close watch over Casey Blue.

'Why do I feel as if you're guarding me?' Casey said teasingly as the detective accompanied her and Storm to the collecting ring. 'I'm not complaining. I like having my own personal bodyguard, but I'm wondering if you know something I don't. Should I be worried?'

McLeod grinned up at her. 'Casey, as you are perfectly aware I'm only pretending to be your minder in order to get up close and personal with the stars. How else would I get a ringside seat to see you and Storm?'

Casey smiled back but he saw doubt flicker across her face.

'What is it? What's wrong?'

She pulled up Storm. 'Lenny, can I say something to you in confidence?'

'Of course.'

'Mrs Smith told me that she'd spoken to you about Ray Cook. I'm not sure how much you know about what went on at Rycliffe Manor but to cut a long story short I was threatened when I left. I've tried to push it out of my mind to focus on Burghley, but now that I'm here it's like a shadow hanging over me. Last night Peter caught a glimpse of someone creeping around Storm's stable-block. I haven't said anything to anyone but it's been eating away at me. I wouldn't put it past that man to try to hurt us – hurt Storm.'

McLeod put a hand on Storm's neck. 'Casey, this is the last thing you should be thinking about when you're about to do dressage. I'm not dismissing your fears. Far from it. I hear you loud and clear. At the same time, I want you to relax and trust that I have your back. Can you do that?

This time Casey's smile was genuine. 'Yes, I can.'

'Good. Now go out there and do what you do best.'

It was 2.55 p.m. when Casey entered the arena. The stands were packed with thousands of people and millions more were watching her live on television and yet as she cantered into the dressage court she'd seldom felt more nervous. It was only after halting and saluting the judges that she remembered Mrs Smith's words. Nothing mattered but the here and now. Nothing was more important than connecting to Storm.

Casey and Mrs Smith had taken a gamble with Storm, not entering him in a single event in the lead up to Burghley. They'd reasoned that it was more important that he arrived at the event completely sound than with extra competition experience. As she changed the rein in a medium trot and guided him into a shoulder-in-left, Casey knew they'd done the right thing. Storm was one of those rare horses who rose to the big occasion. He drew energy from the crowd. His ears were pricked and he felt elastic.

Mrs Smith had gone through the test with Casey so often that she could almost hear her teacher narrating each movement as she rode. *Half pass left. Track left. Collected trot. Extended trot.*

The crowd melted away. Nothing existed beyond Storm. *Shoulder-in right. Circle right, eight metres. Medium walk. Change the rein in extended walk. Halt. Five step reinback. Proceed in collected canter right.*

A dog barked. Casey felt a rush of panic. The Doberman and Rottweiler were at Storm's heels. She saw again

227

their slavering jaws, the blood dripping from the gash on Roxy's flank.

Storm felt her snatch at the bit and was confused. He forgot about the flying change. When the contact came on again, he was relieved. They moved into a serpentine of three loops. They were bonded again, horse and girl, a spiritual centaur. Applause rippled around the arena. The board flashed Casey's provisional score in red – 45.3, putting her in twelfth place. For today, at least, it was over.

23

ANNA SPARKS SHRUGGED into her air jacket and slipped her bib over the top of it. There was a time when she'd have felt invincible in the lead-up to the cross-country, especially if she'd posted a personal best of 40.3 to lie third behind David Powell and Sam Tide after the dressage, but today nerves roared through her system like ocean waves, building and crashing. Anna didn't mind them. Every rider had them. In a way, they were necessary.

She'd once read an interview with the great Mary King, who'd said that she was never afraid as she waited to start the cross-country. If you were, she told the journalist, you shouldn't be eventing. What she feared most was making a stupid mistake that might let her horse down. 'I think what we're doing is so ridiculous ... '

In spite of herself, Anna laughed. She knew exactly what Mary had meant, but it was good to hear it from a gold medal-winning Olympian. Her own anxiety was all to do with Incendiary. She was petrified of doing him harm, either physically or results-wise. The horse was a champion from the tips of his ears to the finest hair on his glossy tail. The onus was on Anna to bring out the best in him.

She was also nervous of the crowd. The reaction to her dressage performance on Friday had been muted in some quarters and downright hostile in others. Leaving the arena, she'd been subjected to loud booing and catcalls. She hoped that the antipathy towards her didn't spill over during the cross-country and in some way endanger Incendiary. If he was injured and it was her fault, she'd never forgive herself.

Hopping down the steps of the lorry that Casper had loaned her, Anna hurried over to Incendiary. He was tacked up and waiting impatiently with Niall, his groom. To be on the safe side, Anna checked her horse over for the umpteenth time. Running her palm across his muscled chest, she drew comfort from the rhythmic thud of his heart. He was feeling confident about the day ahead even if she wasn't.

Riding to the collecting ring, Anna caught a glimpse of a scoreboard. She felt a stab of guilt. Casey Blue had passed up the opportunity to ride Incendiary and now Anna was nine places ahead of her.

'My advisers think I've lost my mind,' was Casper Leyton's opening remark when he'd called her. 'Having been turned down by one seventeen-year-old rider well known for acting on her emotions, I'm offering my finest horse to another, recently banned teenager. Luckily for you, I happen to believe in second chances.'

Since then, Anna had spent a substantial portion of each day trying to come up with a way to repay Casey. So far she'd failed. Perhaps she always would.

From time to time, she rehearsed a conversation in which she asked Casey if she'd consider going for a coffee or a meal when she was next free, but the chances of it happening were remote. Anna had worked hard to become a better person than the spoiled, ego-maniacal brat she'd been before she was banned, but she couldn't forget Casey's words. 'Once a bitch, always a bitch.'

Maybe Casey was right. Maybe leopards never really changed their spots.

Behind the ropes, Niall signalled to her. Five minutes until her start time for the cross-country. Anna's pulse rate doubled. Incendiary began to bounce like a racehorse. It was an overcast day but quite muggy and his neck was already soapy with sweat. He had the ideal temperament for an eventer. Calm and collected on dressage day and all fire when it came to the cross-country.

As he jogged past the milling crowds, snatching at the bit, Anna couldn't repress a grin. Some riders were

231

scared by hot horses, but not her. Their passion for speed thrilled her.

She was moving towards the start when a woman in a blue baseball cap and olive green Barbour jacket crossed her vision. Her cap was pulled down but her profile and something about the way she moved triggered a memory. As she neared, she threw a glance in Anna's direction. There was something so cheerfully malevolent in the look that a bolt of fear that had nothing to do with the fences to come went through Anna. An instant later the woman was gone, swallowed by the milling crowd.

A strange numbness came over Anna. The scene swam away. In a flash, she was back at Rycliffe Manor. She was in the office, throwing a fit because she was positive that she'd left her diary in her bag behind the desk and it was no longer there. It wasn't valuable, but it contained contact numbers and intimate details that she definitely didn't want shared. On a previous occasion her favourite T-shirt had disappeared from her room in the guest quarters.

After raging at Kyle about the missing items Anna had demanded that the police be summoned. Kyle had listened very patiently and soothed her in that infuriatingly reasonable way of his. He'd promised to replace the diary. At the same time, he'd managed to imply that she was being quite petty, considering that she was a millionaire's daughter and the combined cost of the journal and T-shirt was the cost of a couple of coffees. He also implied that she'd more than likely lost them somewhere else.

Ray had been much more scathing. 'I'm not being funny, but who would steal your diary? Isn't it just an endless stream of lunch dates and shopping sprees?'

In the midst of the row, Anna had noticed Hannah watching her from across the courtyard. The junior instructor was sitting on the edge of the fountain with a book in her hand, the picture of innocence. Right then Anna knew – was a hundred per cent certain – that it was Hannah who'd taken her diary and T-shirt. The girl was obsessed with Kyle. The theft of the diary would presumably give her ammunition by allowing her to pry into the life and secrets of a perceived love rival.

Of course, there was no proof that it was her, and Anna had been so creeped out by the brazen way in which Hannah stared her down that she'd dropped the matter then and there.

But it was the final straw. She'd grown increasingly worried about the effect that being at Rycliffe Manor was having on Rough Diamond. Her gifted chestnut horse seemed to have lost the fiery pride that had made her insist that her father bought him for her. His stable name, Mouse, had once been ironic. Now it summed him up. But who or what was responsible for the change, Anna had never figured out.

With hindsight, she realised that she was equally culpable. Had she cared more about the wellbeing of her horse and less about the pursuit of fame and glory, it might be Rough Diamond she was riding at Burghley and not Incendiary, who belonged to Casper Leyton and would never be hers.

At the time, however, the thing she kept returning to was a comment made by Ray soon after Rough Diamond arrived at Rycliffe Manor. 'He has the potential for greatness, your horse, but he needs to be taken down a peg or two.'

Following the stolen diary incident, Anna had made plans to tell Kyle that she was changing teachers. Tragically, that came too late for Rough Diamond, who melted down the following weekend. That, for Anna, had been the beginning of the end – in more ways than one. Such had been the catalogue of woes that followed that Hannah and her stalker tendencies had been the least of her concerns.

' ... Anna Sparks riding Casper Leyton's Incendiary,' the Burghley announcer boomed.

The clock was ticking. Anna's limbs were weak. She was in no condition to manage the stallion plunging beneath her.

The look that Hannah had given her ... it was triumphant. More than that, it was evil. What if it hadn't been Ray who was responsible for robbing Rough Diamond of his confidence and driving him to a breakdown? What if it had been Hannah, the person who routinely exercised the horse? What if it was all part of her plan to rid Rycliffe Manor of her perceived rival? If so, it had worked. She'd destroyed Rough Diamond and driven Anna away. Those two things had set in motion a chain of events that had ultimately almost ended Anna's career.

Could she be planning to come after Anna again? But no, why would she do that? Anna was no longer a threat to her. Casey Blue, on the other hand, was. If there was even a hint of a flirtation between her and Kyle, Hannah's paranoia would magnify it. Anyone capable of stealing, lying and destroying a horse in order to rid Rycliffe Manor of one rival for Kyle's affections, would have no qualms about doing it to another girl, especially since she'd never been caught. Casey was about to compete in one of the most dangerous events in the world. If Hannah decided to try something wicked, the consequences could be catastrophic.

The countdown had started. 'Five, four, three ... '

'Niall!' screamed Anna. 'Niall!'

The groom flew to the ropes. 'What the heck's going on? You're about to be eliminated.'

Anna leaned down. 'This is a matter of life and death. Get an urgent message to Peter Rhys or Angelica Smith. Tell them that they need to stop Hannah Morley. She's on the cross-country course and I think she's out to get Casey. They'll know what to do.'

Giving Incendiary his head, she was gone in a blur.

24

ELSEWHERE IN THE genteel environs of Burghley jazz musicians in boaters and candy-striped jackets entertained the crowds, oblivious to the unfolding drama. Beneath a pewter sky, armies of horse-crazy teenagers in a uniform of polo-shirts, skinny jeans and brown Ariat boots scoured the tented village for tack and clothes. Anyone over the age of eighteen tended to dress in identical tweed and Barbour jackets, with assorted spaniels, chocolate Labradors and wire-haired terriers as accessories. They buzzed like bees around the portable show jumps, Rolex watches and garden furniture.

As the time came for the leading riders to tackle the cross-country course, almost everyone filtered out across the park to stake their claim to the best spots beside the scariest fences. Disregarding the weather, they spread picnic rugs and dug out cameras, binoculars and flasks of coffee. It promised to be a spectacular afternoon of action. As always, the cream of equestrian talent had risen to the top of the scoreboard.

Naturally, people rooted for their favourites. There was the Andrew Nicholson camp and the William Fox-Pitt camp. Others adored Mary King for her humility, intuitive riding and the way she always put her horses first. There were those who argued over whether the Australian, Sam Tide, was better than the American, Stella Blackmore, or if the German, Michael Jung, topped them all. Others vowed they would be Pippa Funnell fans for ever.

When it came to Anna Sparks and Casey Blue, opinion was divided. Many considered Casey to be a flash in the pan. There was no doubt that her achievements were phenomenal but they claimed it was mostly to do with her good fortune in stumbling across Storm, her wonder horse. Casey's devoted followers, on the other hand, insisted she was the most talented British youngster in at least a generation.

The most heated debates were reserved for Anna Sparks. Which side people came down on largely depended on whether they believed in forgiveness or considered her beyond redemption. Either way, they were looking forward to seeing how Incendiary coped with Burghley's unique demands.

The stage was set for a virtual banquet of eventing

spills and thrills. As the clock ticked relentlessly, the tension mounted.

Few in the park were quite so tense as Casey Blue. As planned, she and Storm had begun cross-country day with their own version of eventing's long-format roads and tracks section. Now Casey stood with Mrs Smith, Peter and a British Eventing official waiting for the vet to deliver his verdict on Storm's fitness to continue. A fail would mean automatic elimination.

'Sound as a bell,' he said at last. 'You say that an MRI scan revealed that, like Seabiscuit and Pharlap, the great racehorses, Storm's heart is almost twice the size of a normal horse? Here's why that's a good thing. He's as cool as a cucumber after his morning's work. You'd think he'd done nothing more energetic than stroll over here from the lorry park.'

Casey and Mrs Smith hugged jubilantly. So far, so good.

Peter boosted Casey into the saddle and she rode to the collecting ring with McLeod at her side. It was a sensible precaution but one both viewed as unnecessary. Reassured by the detective, who was of the opinion that the attack on Storm was opportunistic and a one-off, she had put it firmly out of her mind. Her only thoughts were to do with lines and stride counts. She'd walked the course four times and knew it inside out.

'Big and bold,' was how William Fox-Pitt had described it in a television interview. 'It's what Three-Day Eventing is all about. But it tests you mentally and physically. When you walk it, it feels one way. Riding it can be totally different.'

Ruth Edge was more succinct. 'There is no room for error.'

Casey was determined to get a positive start. Setting off tentatively led to time faults. She knew from experience that unless they burst from the D box with intention and intensity, Storm would be in a backwards frame of mind. They had to shave off every available second or finish nowhere. It was that simple. But if they could end the cross-country phase in the top ten or, at worst, the top twenty, there'd be everything to play for on Sunday.

There were thirty-three fences, making thirty-nine jumping efforts in total. As Casey warmed up, Peter and Mrs Smith hurried out to the tenth fence. They hoped that from there they'd also be able to catch a glimpse of Casey at the eighth and ninth and have time to get to the thirteenth in time to see her fly over the fourteenth and fifteenth too.

Casey's father, Roland, and Ravi Singh, his boss and friend from the Half Moon Tailor Shop, were already in prime position at fence twenty-six, the Anniversary Splash. From there they could see the famous water jump. They'd driven up from London first thing that morning and had already seen two dunkings and a run-out.

Provided no one was hurt, watery falls could be amusing, but Roland Blue didn't want any kind of tumble for his daughter. Always anxious when Casey was riding, he grew steadily more nervous as her start time neared.

First, though, came Anna Sparks, Casey's rival. Roland was half-expecting a reprise of her Badminton debacle – a ditching in muddy water, followed by a temper tantrum and a flailing whip. But the girl riding the glorious cocoa-coloured horse looked nothing like the teenage glamour puss he remembered. He had to check the programme to be sure it was her. Anna and Incendiary came pounding down the bank and had cleared all three jumping efforts and splashed out and away before he could blink. The lake was no more challenging to them than a puddle.

'Peter, wait!'

Midway to the ninth, Mrs Smith paused. A wave of agony rippled through her. Despite promising to keep Casey apprised of the most minuscule deterioration in her health, she had not told her pupil that the tablets – even near-lethal doses of them – had stopped working more than ten days earlier. Now when the pain came rolling in it was like a tsunami. It crushed her, leaving her drained.

But that was not the only reason Mrs Smith slowed for a breather. Her heart was racing alarmingly fast. Conscious of Janet's warning about the stimulant properties of the special potion, she thought it prudent to take a rest.

Instantly, Peter was at her side. 'Angelica, what's wrong? Here, lean on me. Are you feeling dizzy? Let me call for an ambulance.'

The pain subsided as suddenly as it had come on. Mrs Smith was so grateful she could have cried. 'For goodness' sake, Peter. You're as bad as Casey. I'm not made of glass, you know. I merely needed to catch my breath. I'm quite fine now. Shall we go? Casey will be starting in a few minutes.'

Peter stood without moving. 'Yes, and Casey would murder me if she thought that I'd allowed you to watch her ride when you were ill and needed help. Please, Angelica. Be sensible. You can watch Casey on TV later. Let me call for the on-course paramedic. That's what they're there for.'

But as he took his phone from his pocket, it started buzzing. The number came up as unknown. Peter answered it without thinking.

'Peter? This is Kyle West.'

Peter was one of the most easy-going people on the circuit, but immediately he was fuming. 'I have nothing to say—'

'This is an emergency, not a social call. I couldn't get hold of Angelica Smith and you are the only other person

I can think of. I found your number on your website. There's this girl at Rycliffe Manor, a junior instructor called Hannah Morley. I've been out of town. I returned last night to find that no one has seen Hannah since Thursday when she went to visit a sick aunt. Her clients are furious.'

Mrs Smith was looking at Peter quizzically. He pulled a face. 'That's fascinating, Kyle, but I have to go. Casey's about to start.'

'Peter, Casey may be in danger. If you care about her, you'll listen to me.'

Peter went cold. 'I'm listening.'

'A few hours ago I asked a friend of Hannah's to check her room in the staff quarters. She found a missing diary belonging to Anna Sparks, piles of newspaper cuttings about Casey with hateful things written on them and a detailed plan of the cross-country course at Burghley.'

'Kyle, we don't have all day. What are you trying to tell me? What's the emergency?'

'My Dad, Ray, he's had a look at the drawings and he's certain Hannah's planning some sort of attack ... I've just arrived at Burghley now, but ... '

A lanky boy in jodhpurs and a sweat-drenched polo-shirt came tearing up to Peter, gasping for breath. 'I've ... been ... looking ... everywhere for you ... Incendiary's groom, Niall sent me ... Message from Anna Sparks. Life and death, apparently. Anna says you need to stop Hannah somebody or other before she gets to Casey and that she thinks she saw her on the cross-country course.'

Peter thanked him and gripped the phone. 'Kyle, can you give me a detailed description?'

A minute later he called McLeod. The detective was planning to watch Casey ride from the media centre, where he could see every fence on television.

'Peter, we've run out of time.'

'What does that mean?'

'It means that Casey is on TV right now. She and Storm are on their way to the start. If something's going to happen, there's nothing we can do to prevent it. We can only hope for the best and respond.'

25

WHY AM I doing this?

That was what Casey was thinking as she waited, reins in hands, poised over Storm's withers, for the starter's countdown. She was supposed to be having fun, but she was terrified. It wasn't that she was terrified for herself. The thirty-three fences that faced her were no picnic, but she trusted Storm to carry her over them safely. He'd never been fitter, stronger or more responsive. But she was terrified for him. What if she made an error of judgement that brought Storm down? What if he broke a leg and had to be put to sleep?

'... The youngest ever winner of the Badminton and Kentucky Three-Day Events, Casey Blue, riding her own Storm Warning ...'

244

'Five seconds,' said the starter.

Casey touched the rose brooch in her breeches pocket and consigned every negative thought to the past. Nothing was more important than the next eleven minutes and twenty seconds, the optimum time for completing the course. Mrs Smith's training schedule, though unconventional, had produced textbook results. Storm was as ready as he'd ever be. Tensed beneath her, he was a coiled spring. With a second to go, she squeezed his sides. He surged forward with such power that Casey had to grab his mane to stay with him. The first fence vanished beneath them. The cross-country had begun.

Some riders measured every inch of the course with a wheel in order to plot the most precise stride counts and lines. Casey and Mrs Smith used the old-fashioned method. Four of Casey's strides equalled one of Storm's, and two long strides for her was roughly where Storm would land after a fence. For the most part, though, they relied on strategy. In a race against time the clock mattered most.

Casey cut the corner to the second, a wooden bench. She settled Storm into a comfortable gallop as they approached the third, a big, solid picnic table guaranteed to make him pick up his feet and start thinking. She'd noticed that a lot of horses veered slightly towards the nearby lorry park as they approached it, so she tapped Storm on the shoulder with her whip as a reminder that she was there. It was unnecessary. He never wavered.

After each fence, she pushed Storm on the instant his

feet touched the ground. 'Moving on quickly when you touch down can save you fifteen to twenty seconds a round,' Mrs Smith was always telling her. So ingrained were her teacher's words that it was as if she and Casey's mum were riding post, guiding Casey and Storm, protecting them.

Casey glanced at her stopwatch. One minute gone.

That morning, she'd watched Ruth Edge, Michael Edge and a couple of others do the cross-country to see how the fences were riding. Fence four was a Burghley classic, a big rolltop followed, two strides later, by a drop down a steep bank. Casey rode it with Mary King's words in mind. 'The art of riding is to be as quiet as possible on your horse. If you keep changing gears, you're going to use up a lot of energy.'

It was a scary fence and required her to be brave as a rider. If she hesitated, Storm would doubt himself. Knowing that when he landed on the downslope he'd have lots of forward impulsion, she condensed his stride as they approached. Head up and shoulders back, she let the reins slip to allow Storm to stretch and get a good look at the skinny coming up. The last thing she wanted was a run-out. Urging him on with her legs and voice, she breathed a sigh of relief when it was over.

The Elephant Trap, she chose to take at an angle. That way Storm was already in position for the turn when he landed. Hands light on the reins, Casey galloped towards the seventh. The first element was a narrow trunk on the rear side of a ditch – an optical illusion that carried the potential for disaster. Storm wasn't fazed. Nor did he mind the brush fence shaped like a Land Rover. One stride then a ditch, three strides then another brush. The angles were daunting but it rode fairly enough.

It was as she steadied Storm for the Cascade Complex ninth that a feeling of dread came over Casey. She could see, as if she were watching it at the cinema, her silver horse rearing, twisting and overbalancing. She saw herself being crushed beneath him. Her reins slackened. The sky seemed momentarily to darken.

Feeling the contact go, Storm scrambled over the oxer. Casey tried to get her thoughts together, but her confidence had evaporated. The trees that preceded the looming Trout Hatchery were threatening. The jolly, cheering throng lining the ropes offered no protection at all. *They* didn't have to negotiate the pond ahead. That was the thing about riding cross-country. There was nowhere more exposed and few places as lonely.

Casey was not the only person having premonitions of doom. McLeod, Peter and Mrs Smith were each doing whatever they could to find Hannah. Unfortunately, they had little to go on. The description they'd been given was hazy at best and since Anna was not a hundred per cent sure that the woman she'd seen was Hannah, there was no way of knowing if she was even at Burghley.

'She might genuinely be visiting a sick aunt,' Peter said hopefully to the young constable McLeod had recruited to help with the search. They were rushing from fence to fence on foot, trying to spot a five-foot-five redhead. Anna had described her as wearing an olive-green Barbour jacket and navy-blue baseball cap.

'Does Miss Sparks have any idea how many people are in green Barbour jackets and blue baseball caps?' panted the constable as they arrived at the water jump to find thousands of eventing fans packing the edges. 'It's like saying that a suspect at a Manchester United game is wearing red and white.'

McLeod, meanwhile, was hurtling across Burghley Park in a Land Rover. Driving dangerously fast, he only narrowly avoided an escaped Jack Russell and a party of picnicking pensioners. Accompanying him was Kyle West, who'd come rushing up to him and said he had a hunch where Hannah might strike if that's what she had in mind. Burghley security had pointed him in the detective's direction. McLeod took one look at him, made a judgement call and they were in the vehicle and racing across the course before Casey and Storm had left the start.

In the crisis, nobody had thought to mention anything to Roland Blue, sitting oblivious with Ravi Singh at the water jump. And Mrs Smith had been left on her own because there was an assumption that she was neither well enough nor fit enough to join in the hunt. In a way, she was glad. The pain had receded, leaving only its

248

ghost, like a bad memory, and for a moment she was almost at full strength.

Peter and McLeod had both walked the course and knew Burghley, but no one understood it with the intimacy of Mrs Smith. She'd not only watched DVDs of every great rider from William Fox-Pitt to Mark Todd winning there, she'd spent a dozen hours wandering it with intent. Every blade of grass was familiar to her, as were all thirty-nine of the jumps designed by Olympic gold-medal-winning Captain Mark Phillips, former husband of Olympic eventer Princess Anne, and father of Zara Phillips, who'd ridden earlier in the day.

After Peter had sprinted away to join the young constable scouring the course for Hannah, Mrs Smith had felt old again. Useless. No good for anything. But then it occurred to her if there was one thing the cancer could not take away from her it was her intellect.

Distant cheers carried on the wind. She glanced at her watch and realised that they were for Casey and Storm, arriving at the start.

'Think, you old idiot!' Angelica Smith ranted at herself. If someone was going to try something in a place packed with tens of thousands of witnesses, where would they try it? Which fence?

She began to hurry towards the trees that crowded the track before the Trout Hatchery. Because, of course, the best place to bring a horse down at Burghley would not be at a fence, watched live by millions of viewers. The easiest place to do it would be somewhere invisible

249

to the cameras and of no interest to the spectators. A spot where the dappled light danced and the shadows shifted and the rider was, for a second, disoriented.

As Mrs Smith half-hobbled, half-ran, Janet's special potion sloshed through her veins with increasing intensity. Her heartbeat began to increase.

When the sirens announced a stoppage on the cross-country course, Casey did not feel the frustration she normally would have at being halted in mid-flow. In fact, it was a blessing. It gave Storm a breather and allowed her to get a grip on herself before tackling the Trout Hatchery fences.

'Any idea what's happened?' she asked a marshal.

'A fall most probably – not at a fence, strangely, but in the trees up ahead. Saw a Land Rover go tearing in.'

Casey shivered. She wondered if the fall she'd imagined had been a premonition, but about another rider not herself.

An animal scream reverberated from the trees. Storm's head shot up.

'Good grief. What was that?' cried the marshal.

Casey was too busy calming Storm to reply. 'Easy, boy. It's only a bird. Nothing to worry about.' As she spoke, the Land Rover emerged and sped away. Tinted windows hid the occupants.

Shutting both the vision and the scream from her mind, Casey eased Storm into a trot. When the signal came to start, she was mentally ready. Sensing that she was with him once more, Storm felt the same way. He raced through the trees without incident, plunged strongly into the pond, over the Goose Nest and duck and then they were off and galloping.

Ahead were two fences that Casey knew would be a challenge. The first was the fifteenth, a huge white oxer. Walking the course, Casey had measured the back rail and found that it was level with her shoulder.

'It's the type of fence that sorts the brave rider from the less cautious one,' Mrs Smith had told her. 'And believe me, there is a difference. In that way, eventing's come full circle. For a while it became a little disappointing because all the emphasis was on show jumping and dressage. Now the courses are more technical and we're seeing the return of chunky, solid fences that ask the big questions.'

The fifteenth was nothing if not chunky and solid. It was arrived at via a red and white house and a post and rails with a drop. Galloping towards the oxer, which grew more intimidating with every step, Casey concentrated on not getting in Storm's way. He trusted her never to take him over an obstacle he couldn't handle. Now she had to trust him.

As he soared into the air, Casey was conscious of wanting to freeze-frame the moment and hold onto it for eternity. She was no longer afraid. Free of gravity and earthly constraints, she wanted only to savour the breeze in her face, the power and grace of the incredible horse beneath her and the upturned faces of the crowd that willed them on. It was as if she'd stepped through a portal into her childhood dream. Storm was the horse of fire she'd always wanted. A horse with wings.

For the remaining five and a half minutes of the cross-country, she saw everything through that rose-tinted filter. Not that it made the fences any less terrifying. The dreaded Cottesmore Leap, the largest eventing fence in the world, presented itself like an obstacle from a nightmare. As Storm flew over the enormous brush, Casey looked down and saw the ditch that followed – a cavernous expanse wide enough to drive a Land Rover through.

Mrs Smith had insisted that the fence was a 'rider-frightener' – scary to people but not to horses and so it proved. Storm sailed over it with barely a pause but swished his tail crossly on landing, as if to say, 'I can handle that, no problem, but I'm not going to pretend I like it.'

As always, Casey found the water jump more enjoyable afterwards than it was splashing through it with thousands of people waiting (some hopefully) to see if she'd come crashing down in the mud. As they galloped towards Burghley House with a whole ten seconds in hand, Casey couldn't stop smiling. A wall of sound came at them as they swept into the arena. Storm cleared the flower table and leapt through the final arch to ecstatic cheers.

There were many riders still to go so it was not until Storm had been rewarded with treats, hosed down with iced water, massaged, rehydrated and had his magnetic rug put on that it was confirmed that Casey was in eighth place after the cross-country, seven spots ahead of Anna Sparks.

26

AT AN HOUR considered unreasonable even by the standards of the early-rising equestrian community, Casey and Mrs Smith sat wrapped in a tartan blanket drinking chai made with cinnamon and honey. They huddled together watching the rising sun stain the sky with a peachy glow. At the far end of the lorry park there were the first stirrings of life, but here they had only the morning star for company.

'I take back everything I said about the Equi-Flow lorry,' said Mrs Smith. 'I would have killed for a soft bed this week. The sofa in this rented one would have been welcomed in medieval times as an instrument of torture. I've left you some money in my will and I want you to put it towards a decent lorry. No, I don't want to hear any protestations. At the very least buy one that allows you to get a decent night's rest.'

She sipped her tea.

'Whatever happened to Ed Lashley-Jones and Candi and Mandi, anyway? I thought you were being sued for breach of contract.'

'I was,' said Casey. 'But that was before he discovered that Anna Sparks would be riding Casper Leyton's best horse at Burghley and decided that it was the business opportunity of the decade. My lovely lorry has been repainted and Anna's using it this week. I miss the cappuccino machine and the soft bed, but apart from that she's welcome to it. Good luck to her. As far as I'm concerned, not enough great things can happen to Anna Sparks. From what Peter says, she provided the description that helped you, Detective Inspector McLeod and Kyle save us from a horrific fall.

'And Ray helped too, because he was the one who made the link between Hannah's drawings and the likely location of the tripwire. Can you believe that? Ray, of all people. And there I was convinced that Hannah was harmless while Ray was only one step away from being an axe murderer.'

'Like I'm always telling you, never judge a man until you've walked a mile in his boots,' said Mrs Smith.

'Yes, but he didn't exactly help himself. He was sinister and aggressive.'

'Now you know the reason for it.'

'Now I do,' agreed Casey.

She did and not a thing was the way she'd imagined it to be. It was a long and tragic story, but it explained a lot. Ray had grown up as an orphan in a community of travellers, being passed from one family to another and knowing little about his own except that his father had been a horse breeder who'd vanished before he was born.

As a young man he had a tremendous gift with horses, but his brusque manner and disfigured face made it difficult for him to progress as a trainer. In the yards where he worked for peanuts he slipped steadily into alcoholism. His wife abandoned him. But his problems were only beginning. When Kyle was about six years old, Ray hit a child while driving in a whisky-fuelled rage and she later died.

Devastated, Ray vowed never again to touch a drop. Not wanting Kyle's life to be ruined by his mistake, he changed both his own name and his son's and told Kyle to tell everyone he met that his father was dead. To pay the bills Ray retrained as an electrician, but he still dreamed of working with horses. When Kyle started failing his riding instructor course, Ray saw his opportunity. Kyle was blessed with charm and good looks, while Ray had the equine knowledge and experience. Together they made an unbeatable combination.

'It was all working perfectly until the pressure of keeping up the deception caused Ray to start drinking again after fourteen sober years,' Casey told Mrs Smith. 'Added to which, they became victims of their own success. People started to ask difficult questions. Kyle was passed over for the Golden Horseshoe Award because the judges wanted more details on how he went, overnight, from being the worst student on his course to being a star instructor.

'Whisky made Ray aggressive and that's the reason he threatened me on the day I discovered their secret. Apparently, he signed up for a twelve-step Alcoholics Anonymous programme the next day. He apologised to me about ninety times when we spoke on the phone after the cross-country and said he was glad that he could do some small thing to make it up to me. I told him that preventing me from breaking my neck was hardly small, but he was welcome to do it any time.'

'And what of Kyle?' asked Mrs Smith. 'Did you get a chance to talk to him last night?'

'I did. In a strange way, it turns out that being rumbled as a fake teacher may be the making of him. After our fight, he walked out of Rycliffe Manor and got on the next plane to Greece. He needed to get away from everything, to try to find himself again. He rented a cottage in the Pyrenees and did nothing but walk and read for weeks. In the end he realised that what he wants is to be his own man, out of his father's shadow, and to live his own life. He plans to study architecture. Funny, he says he likes horses but prefers houses.'

What Casey didn't mention to Mrs Smith, or Peter for that matter, is that as she'd stood in a deserted corner of the tented village talking to Kyle, she'd realised that there'd always be a frisson of something between them. It wasn't love and it wasn't the overpowering electrical attraction she felt with Peter. But it was chemistry. Walking away, she'd turned one last time to find Kyle still watching her, his sun-bleached hair falling over his tanned face, his blue eyes crinkling at the corners. She'd decided there and then that it was just as well he was changing careers.

'You were saying,' Mrs Smith said meaningfully. She could always read her pupil like a book.

Casey flushed. 'I ... oh, yes, I was about to say that when Kyle went AWOL Ray started teaching his clients because he didn't want to let anyone down before Burghley. To his surprise, people liked what he did. If all goes well with his recovery, he plans to open a small yard of his own early next year. It's not somewhere I would ever visit, but, you know, it works for some people.'

She stopped. 'Tell me again what happened with Hannah. I was exhausted and in shock yesterday afternoon. It was hard to take it in.'

Mrs Smith took up the story. 'When Ray hired Hannah to be an instructor at Rycliffe Manor, he did so on the basis of the sterling results she'd achieved when she qualified. He had no idea that she'd been expelled from her high school for stalker-type behaviour. Once she met Kyle and became obsessed with him, she became fixated on getting him at all costs. That included stealing stuff that belonged to anyone she thought might be a rival, including Anna Sparks' diary, and eavesdropping on Kyle's conversations.'

'That's why she decided to throw Roxy and I to the dogs?' said Casey with a shudder.

'Not the nicest way of putting it, but yes. She overheard Ray telling Kyle that it would take something extreme to bond Roxy to you in a hurry – a dog that frightened the horse and caused her to look to you for protection, for instance. He'd been at the whisky and it was simply the ramblings of a drunk. Hannah took him literally. It's hard to know whether she wanted to scare you off at that stage or grant Kyle and Ray their wish. She made a point of warning you about the guard dogs so you wouldn't suspect her and then padlocked the main gate so that you'd have no choice but to go down the lane. It was sheer chance that Ray happened to be on his way to feed the dogs when he heard them going berserk.

'Unfortunately, Ray's history made Kyle fear that he was in some way responsible for the attack. His world began to crumble. It also made him think that if his father could do that, perhaps he was capable of worse. You see, the question of how Philippa Temple's brakes came to fail, conveniently handing the role of director of the equestrian centre to Kyle, has never been satisfactorily resolved.'

'Does McLeod really believe that Hannah might have had something to do with the crash?'

'He thinks it's unlikely but not beyond the bounds of possibility. Apparently her father was a mechanic. If she

259

was already obsessed with Kyle, she may have had the motive.'

'What I can't understand is why she wanted to hurt me and Storm. I mean, I was only ever friendly to her. What did I do to deserve it?'

'Nothing. She became obsessed that Kyle was falling for you and was eaten up with jealousy. Then when you rowed with him, she blamed you for making Kyle leave the equestrian centre and, more importantly, her. In her head, they had a relationship. She became determined to destroy you. Her notebooks show that she considered giving Storm colic with mouldy grass cuttings, along with other horrendous things. In the end she settled on a tripwire on the cross-country course.'

'She hadn't counted on you parachuting in like Rambo granny,' said Casey with a grin.

'Hardly. I sort of limped up to her, half-dead with exhaustion, and said: "Young woman, do you really think that's a good idea?"'

'She sprang at me like a wildcat and would, I think, have strangled me with the wire had Kyle and Detective Inspector McLeod not come roaring up in the Land Rover. Kyle had her pinned to the ground in a trice and Lenny calmly handcuffed her. She was quiet enough until they were helping her into the Land Rover, at which point she let out this eerie howl. It was so inhuman it sent chills through me.'

Casey was quiet for a while. 'How can I ever thank

you? Over the last three years you've saved me from falling more times than I can possibly count.'

'Not half as many times as you've saved me.'

The silhouette of a kestrel appeared in the dawn sky, wheeling and dipping. They followed its twisting flight until it landed, unexpectedly, on a fencepost so close that they could see every detail of its pristine white breast, hooked beak and golden hunter's eyes.

'I was like that once,' Mrs Smith said ruefully. 'A wild spirit.'

Casey gave her a squeeze and tried not to think about how gaunt her teacher had become, all skin and brave bones. 'You still are.'

'No, sadly, I'm not. I'm a bird trapped in the prison of my own body, caged by pain.'

Casey felt a fathomless rage and hurt. How could the sun still rise when the best person she had ever known was slipping away from her, hour by hour. 'On Monday, when this is over, I promise I will search the country – the world if I have to – and find you the finest cancer specialist in existence. If it's humanly possible to cure you, we'll do it. Hey, it's got to be easier than trying to train a teenager who can barely ride to win Badminton on a one dollar horse.'

Mrs Smith laughed. 'If only that was true. No, Casey,

you and I both know that one day soon it'll be over. When that happens I want you to promise me one thing.'

'What's that?'

'That you won't be sad.'

Hot tears filled Casey's eyes. 'How can I promise you that?'

'Because, dear Casey, through you and Storm I've lived. Through you I've dreamed. And, most importantly, through you I've loved. I will go from this world more fulfilled and content than any one person has a right to be, knowing that I'd do it all again twice over if I could.'

Casey could contain herself no longer. Sobs wracked her body as she hugged the teacher she adored, and to whom she owed everything. 'So would I, Angelica. So would I.'

27

'ANNA, WAIT.'

A hazy Sunday morning of pinks and golds had given way to a crisp blue autumn afternoon when Anna Sparks heard Casey call her name. She was on her way to the collecting ring. The combination of a superb horse and the praise she'd received for her performance at Burghley had boosted her confidence and there was much of the old Anna in her coiffed hair, stylishly cut show-jumping jacket and the queenly set of her shoulders. She halted Incendiary. 'Hi, Casey. How's it going?'

'Good, I think.' Casey ran a hand through her riot of dark hair. She hadn't yet changed and was still in ripped jeans and a baggy sweatshirt. 'Anna, I wanted to thank you. What you did yesterday – giving a message to

Niall right before you started the cross-country, that was pretty phenomenal. I guess you've heard about Hannah's arrest. If you hadn't sent word to Peter when you did, they might not have stopped her. Anything could have happened to Storm and me.'

Anna smiled, moving easily with her muscled giant of a horse as he jogged on the spot. 'It was nothing. You'd have done the same.' She checked her watch and gathered her reins. 'Have to dash. I'm jumping at 2.30 p.m. What time are you off?'

'Shortly after three. Good luck.'

'Same to you.' Anna nudged Incendiary and they walked away down the track.

'Hey, Anna.'

The hoofbeats continued but she turned to look over her shoulder. 'Yeah?'

It was on the tip of Casey's tongue to say, 'Win or lose, when this is over would you like to go for a coffee some time?' Then reality kicked in. She and Anna could never really be friends. Their values and their worlds were too different. It was easy to be humble when you were down. When fame and temptation returned, as was surely inevitable, and when she was reunited with her cunning, manipulative father and all his millions, it remained to be seen which of the two Annas would emerge stronger.

'Nothing,' said Casey. 'See you on the other side.'

'See you on the other side.'

Casey was on her way to the lorry park when she

bumped into Niall, who'd nipped back to collect something. A gangly man in an impeccably ironed shirt and breeches, Incendiary's groom had a permanent air of worry.

'Hope Incendiary goes well this afternoon,' Casey said cheerfully. 'Oh, and Niall, thank you for making such an effort to get Anna's message to Peter yesterday. It helped. You've no idea how much.'

Niall's brightened. 'No problem. Glad to do it. I just feel a bit sorry for Anna who's had it in the neck from Casper. She hasn't said a thing about you, but he watched the replay on the telly and saw that something was amiss at the start. Went ballistic. Says she'd be in contention for the title had she not incurred time faults.'

Casey stared at him, confused. 'But I thought she gave you the message before she got to the D box. Are you saying that the countdown had begun?'

Niall became agitated. 'Look, I shouldn't have said anything. It was only a few seconds. Eleven. It's meaningless in the grand scheme of things. If you lose time in cross-country, you make it your business to gain it back again. That's what Anna did. If anything, it probably galvanised her into trying harder. She rode as if there was no tomorrow. If she jumps clear this afternoon, yesterday will be forgotten. Casper doesn't hold grudges. All he cares about is results.'

At 3.05 p.m. Casey rode Storm into an arena packed to capacity with a crowd high on excitement. Already that afternoon several big names had come to grief, while Anna Sparks, who many had privately hoped would clock up a record number of faults, had ridden a flawless round to shoot up to fourth place on the scoreboard. Sam Tide, everyone's favourite Australian, was currently occupying the top spot, with David Powell and Sarah Evershaw lying second and third.

Up in the BBC commentary box, Hugh McFurlough was reeling off some show-jumping statistics for his viewers.

'The governing body of the sport of horse trials, the FEI, states in its rulebook that there should be fourteen to sixteen jumping efforts, no higher than 1.25 metres and no wider than 1.65 metres. What I find fascinating, ladies and gentlemen, is that the course can be no more than 600 metres long and must be ridden at a minimum of 375 metres per minute. Is it just me or is that not worthy of a gold medal in its own right? I mean, it's not as if a horse comes with a speedometer. I find it hard to keep to the speed limit in my BMW. In case there are any policemen listening, it's difficult but I manage it, okay? But a horse is a wilful creature. I'm reliably informed that a horse in the show-jumping arena has a normal stride of 3.65 metres. Does anyone have a calculator ... ?'

He peered from his window and saw Casey and Storm enter the arena as Andrew Hoy left.

'I must say I'm somewhat relieved to have a diversion, and what a pleasant diversion it is. Casey Blue, the youngest ever winner of the Badminton Horse Trials and Kentucky Three-Day Event, riding Storm Warning, the grey she famously rescued from an East End knacker's yard. Not yet out of her teens – she'll be eighteen next week – Casey has taken the eventing world by storm, if you'll excuse the pun. What's nice is that, in spite of her success, she has remained down to earth and likeable, which is more than I can say for some other young athletes I've met in my time ... but, of course, one shouldn't compare.

'She's also very close to her father, which I think is lovely. Roland Blue designed the magnificent show-jumping jacket she's wearing this afternoon as well as her dressage coat and tails. Quite classy, you'll admit. Roland had one or two troubles in years gone by, but he has since become a tailor of some renown. I have before me a press release that says he'll be launching his own line of tailored performance clothing in the run-up to Christmas. Half Moon Equestrian, it's called. Best of luck to him. I'm sure Casey's very proud.'

Below the commentary box, Storm was cantering slowly around the perimeter of the arena, ears pricked, taking in the vibrantly coloured show jumps, expectant faces and buzz of anticipation.

'And now to the business at hand,' continued McFurlough. 'You don't need me to tell you that one of the reasons you can barely fit a pin between people in the stands today is that everyone who can afford a ticket wants to watch Casey Blue and her wonder horse, Storm Warning. Can they pull off the triple by adding the Burghley Horse Trials to her Badminton and Kentucky crowns?

'The Rolex Grand Slam is worth 350,000 dollars to the winner and is a feat only ever achieved by one rider, Pippa Funnell. Relatively speaking, Casey is a long way back in eighth place. She would have to ride a perfect round, especially since there are several seasoned champions still to go. But we're getting ahead of ourselves. There's the bell now. I don't know about you but my heart is hammering so loudly that I can barely hear myself think. Can Casey Blue do the impossible?'

28

RIDING TO THE collecting ring, Casey had been such a bundle of nerves that she'd dismounted in the shade of a lime tree and stood for several minutes with her face buried in Storm's shoulder. Breathing in his wonderful horse smell and remembering why she was there and what was important calmed her. But after a while, he shoved her with his nose as if to say, 'Are we trying to win this thing or not?'

And Casey had laughed as she mounted him, because although Storm was no longer the skeletal wreck she'd rescued and instead resembled a horse out of a George Stubbs masterpiece, all fire and sinew, he still had the same big heart and unquenchable spirit that had made her fall in love with him in the first place.

'What do I do?' she'd asked Mrs Smith. 'If the impossible happens, what do I do?'

'The same thing you always do,' said her teacher. 'Follow your heart.'

Now, as she cantered around an arena so silent you could have heard a mouse tiptoe, Storm's strength communicated to her as if by osmosis. She felt both peaceful and passionately determined. Victory was within her grasp; she just had to fight for it.

From the first jump, she knew that something special was unfolding. Once show jumping had been Storm's weakest phase. Thanks to Mrs Smith's innovative methods, it had become his second strongest after the cross-country. Creating their own version of the long format had taken the edge off his sometimes frenetic energy, leaving the focus critical for this most unforgiving of phases. Fortunes had been made or lost on the displacement of a single brick. Poised within a whisker of the Grand Slam in 2013, Andrew Nicholson and William Fox-Pitt had both knocked poles to say goodbye to that particular goal.

But for Casey, it was still within reach. With every jump cleared, the tension in the arena increased. In the end virtually every spectator was screaming silent screams, willing rattled poles to stay airborne, praying that Storm would lift his feet.

'I don't know how much more of this my nerves can take,' whispered Hugh McFurlough as if raising his voice might distract the horse from his mission. 'One more jump to go. Is Casey Blue about to rewrite the history books? Oh, my goodness, she's done it. Storm Warning cleared the wall with room to spare. Look at him accelerate – a testament to his racehorse past.'

He craned forward, trying to get a better view, wishing he could leave his booth.

'We'll wait to have the result confirmed but Casey Blue and Storm Warning have moved to the top of the leaderboard. There are still seven riders to come so we can't get too excited, but I think most people would forgive a little premature celebration. This remarkable young lady is within a whisker of the Grand Slam – of walking into greatness. Half the people here are in tears. It's like the second flood here at Burghley and not, for once, due to the weather.'

He pulled himself together. 'Right, next we have the reigning European champion, Scott Davis. Oh, dear, he's not going to be pleased to have kicked out a pole on the first jump ... '

Leaning forward, he noticed with alarm that Casey was surrounded by a thicket of officials. One was gesticulating as if he was conducting an opera. He hoped that there had not been a rules violation of some kind. The rules people could be the most dreadful, boring sticklers for equestrian law. It would be so tedious if they found some draconian rule, invented by a florid huntsman in the fourteenth century, with which to charge her. The impassioned build up he'd given Casey would be ruined. Apart from anything else, he wanted

271

her to win. He was a big fan and not ashamed to admit it.

His producer cut rudely into his thoughts. 'What the devil are you playing at, McFurlough? Do the viewers not deserve an analysis of Davis's round?'

McFurlough glowered at the rider down below. 'Scott Davis is having a torrid time,' he said nastily. 'I can't imagine what he's thinking.'

Casey stood in the cold shadow of the stand, waiting for the remaining two riders to determine her fate. Storm had been taken back to the lorry park by Peter and Mrs Smith and she felt bereft. This week more than any other, she and Storm had been one when they were competing, almost as if their hearts beat in time and the same blood ran in their veins. Without him she felt incomplete.

Meanwhile in the arena the crowd groaned as another pole went flying. Casey's clear round had earned her a place at the top of the leaderboard, but all afternoon she'd been sure that someone would overtake her, beating her into second or third place. Part of her hoped they would, because that would make everything easier.

Anna Sparks came up to her. 'Congratulations, Casey. You must be over the moon. There's no stopping you, is there? It's almost greedy, your list of achievements.'

She smiled but there was a coolness in her tone reminiscent of days gone by.

'Thanks, but I'm not counting my chickens,' Casey said guardedly. 'There are a lot of great riders who'll be trying to win this afternoon. Congratulations on your round too. You rode superbly.'

'Oh, do you think so? I was pleased with the way Incendiary jumped, but not with the overall outcome. Unlike you, I've never been satisfied with finishing anything other than first. Yesterday was an expensive lesson. If I had to do it again, I'd make very different decisions.'

She walked away, leaving Casey open-mouthed. Leopards and spots came to mind.

Next along was Lucinda Green. 'Great ride today, Casey. How are you feeling?'

'Truthfully? I've been better. It's ... well, it's nerve-wracking, all this.'

Lucinda smiled. 'Tell me about it. Been there, have the T-shirt.'

'Do you ever miss it? The circuit? The road?'

'Yes and no. It's such a trip away from reality. You live in a bubble. It's true that you don't go to an office, but it's a different type of grind. Each horse is different and each day is different because an animal is different every day. You're driving through the night and you're working long hours. It's a very hard way to make money. You've had some success, Casey, but nothing's guaranteed. Tomorrow is another day.'

She looked at her watch. 'Gotta run. Take care, Casey. See you down the road.'

Outside, the crowd was at fever pitch. A refusal had knocked the last rider out of contention. They began to chant. 'Casey, Casey, Casey, Casey ... '

Casey forced one foot in front of the other. It should have been the best moment of her life, but it was the hardest. The roar of the crowd and the afternoon sunlight came at her in a dazzling wave.

A British Eventing official put his hand on her arm. 'Casey, you don't have to do this. It's not too late. There is nothing in the rulebook. We've issued no statement to the media yet. We wanted to give you time to think it over. The trophy engraver's having kittens, but apart from that—'

'Go ahead and tell the reporters and the engraver,' said Casey, pulling away. 'Please, it's fine. Really.'

Casper Leyton blocked her path. 'Casey, I've heard what you're up to and I've come to tell you that you're making the biggest mistake of your life. I know the reason for it and I can categorically assure you that it's not necessary. In fact, I'm ordering you not to do it. It's insane. You are not responsible for another rider's actions. You've ridden your heart out.'

Casey smiled. 'Thanks, Casper, but my mind is made up.'

29

I T WAS LATE September, but the air in Burghley Park that Sunday afternoon was so balmy it could have been July. Only a coppery scattering of leaves and the faintest hint of woodsmoke on the breeze suggested that change was on the way.

In the centre of the arena, the show jumps were being dismantled in preparation for the prize-giving. One word from Casey and the world would be hers, delivered on a silver platter.

'Casey, huge congratulations from everyone at the BBC,' gushed Hugh McFurlough, beaming at her from behind his microphone. 'Any chance of getting your reaction on winning the Burghley Horse Trials and, by extension, the Grand Slam? It's a towering achievement that will stand with some of the greatest sporting victories of all time. It brings to mind— I'm sorry, what did you say?'

Casey took a deep breath. 'Hugh, forgive me for interrupting, but there is about to be an announcement that will confirm that I am neither the Burghley champion, nor have I won the Grand Slam. I believe I've finished third behind Sam Tide and David Powell. Sarah Evershaw and Anna Sparks are fourth and fifth.'

The commentator was flabbergasted. Inwardly, he cursed the rules tyrants who had brought about this calamity. 'I don't understand. There must be some mistake.'

'I wish there was, but there isn't. Yesterday, one of the riders was delayed at the start of the cross-country trying to get a message to me – a message that played a part in preventing a serious fall.

'Even without the delay, that rider would not have won the Burghley Horse Trials, but I could not in good conscience take the trophy today knowing that someone lost eleven seconds and incurred a penalty point because of me. There is nothing in the rulebook that covers this situation, but for me it's a matter of principle. I've asked the British Eventing and FEI officials to add eleven seconds and a penalty point to my score. Once that was done, Sam Tide became the clear winner. I'd like to congratulate him now. He's a fantastic rider and a brilliant ambassador for our sport.'

'Yes, but you had a chance to write yourself into

the record books with the Grand Slam,' protested McFurlough. 'What about the 350,000 dollars? That's over 200,000 pounds.'

'Money isn't everything, Hugh.'

'Of course not but—'

Casey smiled. 'If you have a minute, I have another announcement to make.'

McFurlough moved out of shot to mop the sweat from his brow. 'Take all the time you need.'

'As of this moment, I'm retiring from eventing. I know people will laugh because I'm still in my teens, but age has nothing to do with my decision. The past three years have been more magical, more terrifying and more rewarding than I could ever have imagined. I could not have done any of it without my coach, Angelica Smith, or the support of my boyfriend, Peter, and my dad. At the same time, I've learned a lot about myself. When I started eventing I vowed always to put my horse, Storm, and the people I love before everything else, especially fame and success. At a certain point I found that that was becoming a challenge. This is a beautiful life but it's not without its demands and temptations.'

She stopped, struggling to control her emotions. 'But that's not the main reason for my decision. This week Storm Warning was threatened with serious injury or worse. He was put in that position for one reason only and that's because I was pursuing my goals. He's loved competing as much as I have, but now it's time he has a well-earned rest.'

'But what will you do?' spluttered Hugh McFurlough, who was feeling overwhelmed himself. 'I mean, you're so young. You have your whole life ahead of you.'

'I'm not sure. I'm going to take some time and take stock. A few months ago, I had the opportunity to do some teaching at my old riding school, Hopeless ... apologies, Hope Lane in East London. It made me think that I'd enjoy helping underprivileged kids learn to ride. I'd also love to open a sanctuary to save horses like Storm. I'm not sure where it would be. Peter is from Wales, so maybe somewhere around there.'

Watching at home, Jennifer Stewart cast a pained glance at the cheque sent by the latest buyer to reject her wayward mare, which lay ripped up on her coffee table. 'As difficult as it is for me to admit it, there's only one owner who's really right for Lady Roxanne and that's Casey Blue,' she said to her husband. 'Horses adore her and when you listen to her talk, who on earth can blame them. First thing Monday morning, let's box up Roxy and dispatch her to White Oaks.'

At Burghley, an official signalled to Casey. The prize-giving ceremony was beginning.

For Casey, it was an odd feeling to stand beside Sam Tide in the place reserved for the rider who finished third when she could so easily have been in Sam's shoes, reaching for the trophy. But she didn't have a single regret. If anything, she felt liberated. She was the luckiest girl in the world to have experienced the joy and exhilaration of eventing, but now it was time to let go.

Sam Tide lifted the trophy and beamed for the cameras as the Burghley crowds erupted. Many spectators would have preferred Casey to win, but Sam was immensely popular and they celebrated his victory appropriately.

'I've dreamed of getting my hands on this trophy since I was a boy,' he said into the microphone, 'and that's why I can't believe I'm going to do what I'm about to do. First, let me explain. The aim of most people who ride or play sport for a living is to be as gracious in victory as you are in defeat. I can tell you from experience that's easier said than done. As Casey said in her interview earlier, demands and temptations come at you constantly. It's tough to always do the right thing.'

He wiped his eyes. 'Gosh, this is embarrassing. I haven't cried since my dog died when I was twelve.'

Laughter rippled around the arena.

'But today I witnessed the greatest act of sportsmanship I've ever known. Casey Blue, who had the chance to stand before you not only as the winner of the Burghley Horse Trials but also as only the second person in history to have achieved the Grand Slam, voluntarily called a penalty on herself to show solidarity with a rider she felt had helped her. Because of this selfless act, I am fortunate enough to be your champion. It is a title I gladly accept. But I would like to acknowledge this astounding act of grace and courage with a gift.'

He turned to the girl on his left and handed her the trophy. 'Casey Blue, this one's for you.'

CALLING ALL GROWN-UPS!
Sign up for **the orion star** newsletter to
hear about your favourite authors and exclusive
competitions, plus details of how children
can join our 'Story Stars' review panel.

Sign up at:

www.orionbooks.co.uk/orionstar

Follow us 🐦 @the_orionstar
Find us **f** facebook.com/TheOrionStar